The Notorious Nutcracker Case

The Pearl Hotel Cozy Mystery Series

Book 3

NANCY PENNICK

The Pearl Hotel Mystery Series is dedicated to my sister, Susan, who encouraged me to bring Serena to life. To my cousin, Beth, who always says yes when I ask for help. And, to my husband, Ron, who reads every word I write.

Chapter One

Proud mother syndrome swept through Serena Tate as she listened to her daughters' presentation. She studied the intensity on their faces and realized they had invested their heart and soul into the project. Concluding their noteworthy speech to Nina Takeda, the owner of The Pearl Hotel, they now sat waiting for a response. Their eyes shone with innocence and youth, but proud or not, Serena was about to wipe the excited expressions from their faces.

"No. Absolutely not." Serena folded her arms over her chest.

"Serena," Nina scolded. "At least let me hear them out."

"Thank you, Mrs. Takeda," Jade said.

"Nina, you listened to the girls, as promised," Serena replied. "They gave their presentation, and you've done enough."

"As I was saying." Jade gave her mom a 'do not interrupt me' look. "Jewel and I are taking a marketing class. The professor assigned a project as the final. We must create a plan for an event or business venture and explain how we would market it. It gave us an idea." She turned to her sister. "Go ahead."

"Why not create an actual event? See if our ideas work," Jewel said. "The Pearl's gardens are the perfect spot for the market. It also would benefit the hotel."

When people walked into the main entrance of The Pearl Hotel, the gardens greeted them. Stepping through a red Torii gate, visitors would find a tearoom, sushi restaurant, gift and clothing shops nestled among an authentic Japanese setting. Serena's beloved pond and its stunning fountain sat in the center of the gardens. Numerous paths wound through the beautiful landscape, which ended in secluded cul-de-sacs or led people to various shops and restaurants. This magnificent setting helped The Pearl secure a place as one of San Francisco's top ten attractions.

"Some European countries have an ongoing Christmas tradition," Jewel continued. "*Christkindlmarkt* or Christmas markets originated in the late Middle Ages. Germany held the first open-air market dedicated to the holiday. Eventually, the idea spread to other countries. Germany, France, Switzerland, and Denmark, among others, still hold them to this day." She blew air through her mouth as if she'd finished a workout. "Just a brief history."

"Jewel and I want to expand this concept," Jade said. "She and I would love to set up a booth to sell toys, clothes and music instruments from African nations. The shops in the garden can fill their storefronts with holiday gifts from Japan."

Serena could not contain herself any longer. "Girls, this is an enormous task. It's September. School started a month ago, and you have other classes."

"We'll manage," Jade answered. "I already made a to-do list. Our goal is to invite authentic artists worldwide to join the market. We've found a man in Germany who designs and sells nutcrackers. He's shown interest in the event."

"We learned an Austrian choir practices at our school," Jewel added. "The director moved from Austria to California to teach at the college and created a choir for those of Austrian descent. He once sang in the Vienna Boys' Choir, but his group is open to all singers. I discovered a classical Indian dance class on campus, and the teacher would love to give performances at The Pearl. No need to search far for diversity and talent."

"Great," Serena said. "You've done your homework. How would this person from Germany get here? Do the choir and dancers charge a fee? You girls are over your heads. Sorry to burst your bubble, but you need to hear the truth."

Serena saw the light go out in Jewel and Jade's eyes, and her heart broke. She had seen the look once before in her daughters' lives. It happened the day the twins announced they wanted to become models. Jade, who'd gotten her father's handsome looks and rich brown skin tone, had practiced her walk and poses since she was five. Jewel, who favored Serena, with her honey brown skin and golden-brown eyes, had joined forces with her sister due to her love of fashion and wearing Serena's heels from the same age. Despite their contrasting appearances, the fraternal twins shared common goals. She had shot them down then, just as she did now. Serena had stressed education as their most important aspiration. It hadn't felt good at the time, and today was no exception. She searched her mind for more excuses to ease their pain.

"*High Heels and High Stakes* has just come out, girls. My book tour starts in another week. Although I'd love to help, I won't be here." Serena glanced at Nina for help. "A perfect reason to end this conversation."

"Perhaps not," Nina responded. "Girls, I'd like to see a list of vendors and entertainers. Rooms are available for those who require them."

"Thank you, Mrs. Takeda. We'll get a copy to you this week," Jewel said.

"Nina," Serena hissed. "You are supposed to take my side."

"There are no sides, Serena."

"You can't do this alone." Serena pursed her lips and stared at Nina.

"Who said I would?" Nina nodded toward the entrance of the tearoom.

Serena turned to see her two friends, Mia Takeda and Lily Nichols, headed their way. "How did you…? Never mind. You definitely were a secret ninja in a past life."

Nina's laughter was light and laced with amusement. Serena could only shake her head and admit defeat.

Serena's smile widened as her friends approached. Mia, a renowned fashion designer, and Lily, a tech wizard, held a cherished place in her heart. Judging by their matching enthusiastic expressions, Serena realized Nina had already asked for their help.

"Hi, Jade," Lily said, hugging her, then turned to her sister. "Jewel. How's school?"

"It's going well, but we have a giant project to complete. Jade and I came to the tearoom to give a presentation to Mrs. Takeda. It's part of our marketing class grade."

"So, it's a working lunch," Mia replied. "Grandmother." She turned to Nina. "Have you ordered?"

"We are about to do so, my dear child. Stay. You, too, Lily. Please join us for a relaxing cup of tea before we order."

The tearoom's moss green walls had perfectly spaced cherry wood faux windows. Translucent white paper filled the window's square spaces. Matching rectangular lanterns sat in the middle of each guest's table. The designers had chosen seating from the same rich-colored wood, which cast a reddish glow. They'd placed lifelike cherry blossom trees against the walls and in strategic corners. Vertical wood beams, with gold calligraphy dancing down their centers, created a feeling of being transported to another time or place. Serena usually soaked in her surroundings, but not today. She loved the tearoom's atmosphere, yet she couldn't relax.

"Serena." Lily placed her hand on Serena's arm. "You seem tense."

"I am," Serena said under her breath. "I can't see how they'll complete this by December."

"With our help, they will." Lily winked. "We know people."

Lily spoke the truth. She had married a billionaire who owned a tech company. Mia, hailing from the California Takedas who'd reached billionaire status decades ago, also had a wealthy husband. Until now, their money had never crossed Serena's mind. *Yes, they could help, but I don't want them using their money or connections.* Then she said aloud, "Girls, if you're going to do this, you must do the work. You can't depend on Nina, Lily or Mia to solve your problems."

"I only offered hotel rooms and can write them off as an expense," Nina stated. "I'm also here whenever they need a consultation."

"Lily and I still need to hear their proposal before we offer help," Mia said. "But I understand what you mean, Serena. No throwing money at the project."

"If this is to happen," Serena replied. "I want the hotel to profit."

"Everyone stands to gain," Nina said. "People love the holidays, and the gardens are popular year-round."

"I mentioned the German seller to show there is international interest. People have heard of The Pearl Hotel. It has an excellent reputation," Jade said. "We don't expect many international artists to respond to our call, but if we could get one, we'd be thrilled. Besides, San Francisco has a diverse population we can tap into, and we plan to advertise to colleges in the area. Most students will work for free." She turned to her sister. "Tell them about Carmody, Jewel."

"I met Carmody Fletcher at the school's fine arts showcase." Jewel replied. "His personality is a little overwhelming, but his talent is undeniable. He's a junior and wants to build a portfolio for his future career. Carm will offer his services for free, an opinion shared by many drama and art students alike."

"What would this Carmody fellow do?" Serena asked, raising her brows.

"He has developed a holiday character called Selfie the Elfie." Jewel rolled her eyes. "He should work on the name, but he thinks it explains his character quite well. Carmody would wander through the gardens, greeting visitors and acting as a tour guide, directing guests to booths and shops. He will take pictures with people or offer to photograph their family."

"You already spoke with him and offered him the job?" Serena stared at Jewel.

"Only in general, Mom. He introduced me to some talented people at the show. Most are eager to showcase their work and hope to sell some art."

"You girls have done well," Mia said. "It's already September, which gives us little time. Have you chosen dates for the Christmas market?"

"Markets traditionally run through Advent, the four weeks leading up to Christmas," Jewel answered. "However, we'd condense it into the two weeks before Christmas. By then, the fall semester will have ended."

"Shortening the time is a great idea," Lily said. "If it's successful, you can expand next year."

"Next year?" Serena almost choked on her tea. She coughed and patted her chest.

"Hypothetically, Serena." Lily smiled at her. "It's up to Nina if she wants to continue the event."

Lily removed her tortoise-shell framed glasses and wiped them on the linen napkin. Her light brown hair with blonde highlights fell across her oval-shaped face. Her beauty shone inside and out. She wrinkled her forehead, probably trying to understand why Serena was being so difficult. Although her friends were willing to help the girls, Serena was giving them a hard time. Guilt spread through her.

"I'm sorry I snapped at you, Lily," Serena said, then looked into Mia's rich chocolate eyes. "You, too, Mia. You're only trying to help, and I've fought every suggestion." *I've been too harsh on everyone. The reason? I don't want Nina or my friends to think we're taking advantage of them. I'll speak with Nina and the girls later.*

"Do I get one of those apologies?" Nina asked, with a twinkle in her eye.

Nina, an impressive woman in her mid-seventies, was the matriarch of the Takeda family and kept their Japanese traditions alive. She owned The Pearl Hotel, Serena's home away from home, and commanded attention in any room, despite her height of five feet and one inch. Her chignon bun always appeared neat, and she never had a hair out of place. With her fashion sense, Nina constantly looked runway ready. She had her nails done to perfection, never a chip or the wrong color. But her best trait was loyalty to friends and family, and Serena was happy to be included in that circle.

"I didn't forget you, Nina," Serena replied. "I saved the best for last. Thank you for supporting my daughters. If you approve, who am I to refuse the great Nina Takeda?" she playfully teased. "I'm all in. I'll help in any way I can. We'll make this the best darn Christmas market the world has ever seen."

"I wouldn't go that far," Nina kidded. "I have visited many, and the standard is high."

"We'll reach for it," Jade said.

"We won't disappoint you, Mrs. Takeda," Jewel added, then turned to Serena. "I ordered your favorite almond cookies to thank you for changing your mind."

"We need to eat lunch before the cookies." Serena laughed.

"Haven't you heard of dessert first, Mom?" Jade said. "When we had a tough day, you would say, 'Let's have dessert first.'"

Serena's heart melted. "You had me at dessert first."

Everyone at the table laughed as Jun, their dedicated server, set a two-tiered cookie tray filled with the almond treats and other goodies on the table. "Enjoy," she said. "Can I get anyone more tea?"

"Oolong for me," Serena said. "Thanks, Jun."

"The usual." Jun winked.

"Jun, I order other teas." Serena defended herself, inwardly chuckling at their private joke.

"Of course you do." Jun nodded her head and smiled as she left the table.

As the group passed the dessert tray, Jade said, "We need your help with one more thing." She glanced at Jewel.

"Christmas Market sounds boring," Jewel responded. "Mom, you're the writer. Can you think of a catchy name?"

"Right off the top of my head? No," Serena answered. "But I have an idea. There are six of us here. Why don't we brainstorm?"

"Wonderful idea," Mia said. "What about Season's Greetings Christmas Market?"

"Not bad." Jewel nodded her head.

"Or something whimsical, like Holly, Jolly Christmas Market or Jingle and Joy?" Lily offered.

"Nina," Serena said. "Your turn."

"I am not good at creative ideas." Nina chuckled. "I have a team for that."

"Okay, we'll grant you a pass." Serena tapped her chin. "Here is my submission. Merry and Bright Christmas Market."

"I love it," Jade said.

"I volunteer to make a logo and signs," Lily said. "It will be easy peasy. It's part of what we do at Nicholworks."

"I am happy to help with costumes and design," Mia added.

"That's wonderful!" Jewel exclaimed. "Thank you all."

Serena glanced around the table. "I agree with Jewel. It's wonderful. After what happened this year, we need an enjoyable experience." She smirked. "At least I hope it will be."

"Mom!" the twins said in unison.

"I'm kidding." Serena held up her teacup. "To the Merry and Bright Christmas Market."

Chapter Two

Nina excused herself to attend to hotel business, and the twins departed after receiving a text from their rideshare service. Serena gazed at her two friends, who remained seated at the table, and said, "I'm glad it's just the three of us. I wanted to check in with you. How are you feeling about this project? I'm crossing my fingers for a peaceful Christmas market, but unexpected events took place at The Pearl this year."

"Like a model's murder?" Lily raised her brows. "Then someone killed a gangster's daughter?"

"Yes. Like that." Serena exhaled. "My wish is to use our P.I.C. text alerts for important market updates and nothing else. No murders. No suspects to investigate. No sequestering in the hotel."

"I agree. We are partners in crime for everything in life." Mia said. "We'll help each other solve problems, no matter how small."

"Thank you." Serena blew through her lips. "I feel much better."

"You're under pressure, Serena," Mia said. "Let us shoulder the burden while you're away on your book tour. Enjoy the time. Is it true what I heard?" She wiggled her eyebrows. "Jack is joining you for part of the trip?"

"Mia." Serena glowered at her. "Stop with the eyebrows. You're aware Jack and I are taking things slow."

"Since February?" Lily asked. "Mia, we should talk to him."

"Lily!" Serena turned her attention to her. "Remember what Nina said. Jack's ex hurt him, and it's my guess, he swore off women. I'm taking it slow, as she suggested."

"Serena's right, Lily," Mia replied. "We must let him go at his own pace." She patted Serena's hand and giggled. "I remember when you first met him. You came to me demanding answers about his background, and I knew you had instantly fallen for him."

"What did she ask?" Lily glanced from Mia to Serena.

"The usual things one wants to know. Married, single or girlfriend. Children. Age." Mia lifted her shoulder. "I can't recall the entire conversation, but I remember the light in Serena's eyes. She still has it."

"Obviously, you told her Jack was single and in his mid-forties," Lily stated.

"Yes, and that he was Japanese like me." Mia smiled. "Serena was quite capable of taking it from there. She needed no more information."

"You're a couple now," Lily said. "That's what counts. Once you're away from The Pearl, your ex and your kids, something might happen." She winked.

"We'll see," Serena sighed. A desire to visit the pond and see a certain red koi crept over her. She placed her linen napkin on her plate. "I'll say my goodbyes now. I leave early tomorrow morning."

"How long will you be gone?" Lily asked, rising from her chair to hug Serena.

"Two weeks. I'll visit bookstores in major cities, do some television interviews on those local morning shows, then come home. I can do podcasts from here, and the publisher's interns do the social media marketing. Thank goodness I don't have to create media or ads." Serena shook her head.

"It sounds like a busy schedule," Mia said. "But time will fly. Where will you start the tour?"

"The Big Apple. New York City," Serena answered. "When I have some downtime, Jack and I plan to eat at delis and visit The Statue of Liberty."

"Any romantic activities on that schedule?" Lily asked. "Perhaps a candlelight dinner?"

"I want to walk hand in hand through Central Park," Serena replied. "It doesn't need to be fancy or expensive."

"I'll get you a reservation at my favorite restaurant," Mia said. "I'd like to contribute to the romantic side."

Serena had forgotten Mia and Kade lived in New York City before moving to The Pearl in San Francisco. The couple had met when Mia and her partner, Jordan Reese, were struggling fashion designers. Kade had promised Jordan he'd mentor the pair after seeing their work. Drawn to each other from the start, Kade and Mia had fought adverse odds to be together.

They were meant to be. Serena smiled at her friend. "Thanks. Send me the details." She hugged each friend one last time. "With that, I need to go. I left everything to the last minute—packing, favorite pens for book signings, itinerary for Mama and the girls."

"Luckily, the plane will wait for you," Mia said.

Nina had offered to fly Serena and Jack to New York City on the Takeda jet. Serena didn't want to appear ungrateful, but Nina had already gifted her an office and a suite at The Pearl. She graciously turned down the wonderful gesture. Fly her around the country? That was her publisher's job. Yet in the end, Nina won out, and Serena finally accepted the generous offer.

Serena and Jack would leave in the morning, and the thought of traveling together piqued her excitement. She would finally have Jack to herself on the plane. No interruptions. *The things we could do. No, I'd never... There's a flight attendant and two pilots.* Serena smiled at the imaginary image of what could happen.

"I can't believe they will release your second book in a matter of days, Serena," Lily said. "Seems like yesterday when *Marry Me Never* debuted."

"Now *High Heels and High Stakes* is here," Mia stated. "Did you think you would become a published author when we met two years ago?"

Serena had to agree with her friend. Her life had undergone significant changes since they met. Two years prior, she held two jobs—one in a boring office and the other as a part-time rideshare driver. *Because of the second job, I met Mia. Talk about fate.* Serena had helped her passenger escape a difficult situation, and since Serena dreamed of becoming an author, the narrative had fallen into her lap. She and Mia became friends, and Serena had asked permission to write a fictionalized version of Mia's actual experience. After reading the first draft, Mia had given her approval.

To her surprise, Serena's debut novel became a bestseller. She quit her office job but kept the other. Chauffeuring people around the city seemed to fit her personality. She prided herself on the ability to judge someone's character, and it helped her writing. A notebook always traveled with her, and on the day she befriended Mia, she had hastily written what she had learned inside her treasured journal.

Serena took Mia's hand. "I believe in fate, Mia. Something led me to you."

"I feel the same," Mia said, squeezing Serena's hand. "Have a great time. Send pictures, please."

"Lily?" Serena turned to her other friend. "Thanks for helping the girls."

"I'm looking forward to it. I already have some ideas." Lily embraced her again. "Thanks for letting me read the book before release day. I think it's better than the first one."

"Really?" Serena's eyes filled with tears.

"Yes." Lily squeezed her and stepped back. "Go. You've got much to do."

"You're right. I need to leave before this becomes a hug fest." Serena waved and hurried out of the tearoom, following the flagstone path to her beloved pond. She felt a magnetic pull toward the spot, as if Samurai called to her. "He's a fish, Serena Tate," she said under her breath. But when the red and white koi sprang from the water, her heart leaped with joy. "Sam!"

The red fish with white tail, fins and underbelly swam to where Serena stood. "I brought you treats." She shook the bag filled with honey oat cereal. "Your favorite."

Serena had checked with Nina before feeding the fish. A sign by the pond announced that food was for purchase at the gift shop, but Nina explained it was needed to protect the koi's safety. In fact, they could eat many things, including the correct people food. The cereal, easy to carry in her purse, made the top ten list of what the koi loved to eat.

"I'll be gone for two weeks, Sam." Serena gazed down at the fish. He blinked as if he understood but didn't appear happy. "It will go fast." She let out a long breath. "I don't want to go now. Too much is happening here. Will you watch out for my girls? They'll be visiting the gardens to map out their Christmas market."

Samurai squinted and cocked his head as if to say he didn't comprehend. "I'll sum it up for you." Serena did her best to describe the Merry and Bright Christmas Market to the fish. "I have ideas but don't want to intrude."

The red koi swam in circles and popped up his head.

"Yes, interfere?" Serena and Sam had an understanding. She would ask yes or no questions, and he would respond by popping his head up for yes or showing his tail for no.

"Okay, you think I should speak with them. The girls have returned to school, but I could call them." She headed to a bench opposite the pond and dug out her phone.

"Mom?" Jade answered on the second ring.

"Hi, sweetie, are you at school?" Serena asked.

"Yes."

"Good trip? No creepy rideshare driver?" Serena joked.

"A little." Jade laughed.

"No one tops your mom for great conversation during a ride, if I may be so bold," Serena said with a teasing tone in her voice.

"Jewel and I would rather not talk to the driver, Mom. This woman couldn't stop telling stories. By the time we arrived at the university, we knew her entire life history."

"That sounds interesting."

"Not when she included every surgery she has had," Jade huffed.

Serena refrained from defending the driver, despite her belief that the woman was lonely and had no one to listen to her. "Is Jewel with you?" she asked.

"No, she went to the Fine Arts building to hang flyers. Do you need both of us?"

"Not really. Before I leave, I wanted to share some suggestions about the market."

"Mom."

Serena heard the exasperation in Jade's voice. "I said suggestions, Jade, but they're important ones."

"Fine. Let's hear them."

"I want you to vet each vendor. You know what vet means?"

"Yes," Jade huffed louder. "To investigate and verify their background before asking them to join the project. It's only a market, Mom, but we plan to check out the applicants and make sure they're legit."

"Good. My second suggestion is to have Nina attend the interviews at The Pearl. You planned to hold them there, right?" Serena didn't wait for a response. "Nina gets final say."

"Mom!"

"It's her hotel, Jade. She's putting her reputation on the line for you. We don't want to take advantage of Nina, especially monetarily."

"Okay, anything else?"

"Yes, I'm proud of you. I tried to stop the project because I thought it would overwhelm you. Your education is more important."

"What made you change your mind?" Jade asked.

"I didn't change my mind. I always believed in you."

"I understand."

"Really?"

"You thought Jewel and I were taking the easy way out. Ask Nina for help, and she provides everything we need."

"It crossed my mind."

"We proved you wrong," Jade said in a playful voice, then changed to a more serious tone. "We love Nina. She's family."

"We do love her, don't we?" Serena wiped a tear trickling down her cheek.

"Jewel and I will prove how competent we are to all of you. Don't worry, okay? I've got to go. Time to study."

"Did you say that just for me?"

"Yes."

"Stay in touch?"

"I will. I love you, Mom. Have fun on your trip and don't worry about us. Grandma always checks on us, and we have Mrs. Takeda, Lily and Mia."

"It takes a village." Serena smiled.

"We're grown, Mom, but we love they still watch over us."

"Tell Jewel I love her, too, and will call as soon as I can." After ending the call, Serena hugged her phone to her chest. "I should go home and pack."

Serena rose from the bench and walked to the white Japanese-style fence that surrounded the pond. Leaning on the ledge, she listened to the sounds of the garden, which always calmed her spirit. The fountain sprayed water into the air, and Serena watched as the droplets fell and danced on the surface before becoming one with the liquid. "Good-bye, Samurai. See you soon," she whispered.

* * * *

"Mom?" Serena called from the mudroom. "I'm home."

Robin Baker, Serena's mom, had moved in during the summer to help until the girls left for college. The arrangement had worked so well, Serena asked her to stay permanently. Her mom rounded the corner and met Serena as she entered the kitchen. Their matching brown eyes with flecks of gold immediately connected, and Serena knew trouble lay ahead.

"What is it?" Serena asked.

"You have a visitor," Robin answered.

"Who?"

Before her mom could answer, Justice, Serena's ex-husband, appeared in the doorway. No one could say Serena had poor taste in choosing men. At six foot three, Justice possessed a rugged bad-boy charm, which added to his attractive look. His perfectly trimmed goatee and neatly braided hair looked as if he'd come from the barbershop. Serena checked out his arm muscles, impressed that he stayed in shape. At one time, her heart would have skipped a beat when she saw him. Now she could only think he had ulterior motives.

Serena inhaled and released the breath in a measured manner. "Hello, Justice. What can I do for you?"

Justice cleared his throat. "As I told your mom, I'm here to ask permission to help our girls. Although the twins are adults now and can make their own decisions, I thought I owed you that courtesy."

"Fine. Go ahead. Don't keep me in suspense." Serena narrowed her eyes. "What is this about?"

"The girls told me about their Christmas market."

"When?"

"Today. After they returned to school. They're so excited."

"You just *happened* to call them?"

"No, they called me." Justice shifted from one foot to the other. "Come on, Serena, don't be so hard on me. I want to help them. I'll even take vacation days so I can be available."

"What would you do?"

"Anything that needs to be done. What do you say?" Justice gave her a pleading look.

Serena tried to hold her anger in check, but it was no use. She shouted at him, "No. No. No. A thousand times, no."

Chapter Three

"Isn't that a little harsh, Serena?" Justice took a few steps toward her.

Serena held up her hand. "Stay where you are."

"What's the reason I can't help my daughters? Can you give me a good one?" Justice cocked his head to one side.

Serena and Justice had met as teens and married young. Serena naively assumed it would last forever. He would stare at her with his seductive brown eyes, and she had melted every time. Twenty years later, Serena realized lustful emotions and those beckoning eyes weren't enough to sustain a marriage. The couple never built a solid foundation, and it had crumbled after the girls were born. Justice refused to change his habits or adjust to their new schedule. Serena managed the daily tasks and after-school activities. When Justice began to skip dinners and social events, she had had enough and filed for a divorce.

At twelve years of age, Jade and Jewel hadn't fully understood why their parents parted ways, but Serena and the twins bonded in their determination to make the best of things. Justice saw the girls a few times a year, mainly on Christmas and their birthday. When Serena became a well-known author, Justice suddenly wanted back into her life. After watching the girls walk in Mia's fashion show, Justice suddenly became Father of the Year. To sum it up, she didn't trust him.

Serena shook the memories from her head. "I can give you six reasons, Justice. One for each year you barely saw the girls."

Justice threw out his hands. "I'm trying to repair the damage, Serena. Give me a break."

"I'll ask Nina what she thinks," Serena said. "I can also have her ban you from the hotel."

"You wouldn't do that." Justice hung his head, appearing remorseful.

"No, I'm not that cruel," Serena answered. "But there will be boundaries."

Justice perked up at her words. "Sure. Fine. Whatever you say."

Serena narrowed her eyes. "Tell me. Did you already offer your services to the girls?"

"No. It's the reason I came here. I want your blessing."

"Alright, you have it. You can help them build booths, paint signs or whatever they want done. When the market opens, don't spend the entire day there."

"I can design whatever they want. You've seen what I can do, Serena." Justice paused. "I had planned to stop by daily. What if the girls need a break? I can take over their booth."

Justice presented a good case. Serena had to admit his carpentry skills were wonderful as she'd seen firsthand.

He'd built a dining room table for their first home. Besides his woodworking talent, Justice would make a great bodyguard, even though she convinced herself nothing major would occur at the market. *Enough has happened at The Pearl. What could go wrong?*

"As long as you stay in the background, Justice," Serena answered. "If you try to take over…"

"I won't," Justice quickly said.

"This isn't a done deal," Serena responded. "You can help the girls offsite, but Nina must okay your presence at the hotel."

"Can you speak with her before you leave on your book tour?" Justice gave her a sheepish grin. "I need to measure before I build anything. Jade and Jewel plan to stay in your suite this weekend, and I'd like to meet them at the hotel."

"Hold on here." Serena placed a hand on her hip. "The girls are staying in my suite? They never asked."

"Oh, shoot. There I go again." Justice rubbed his hand over his face. "I said too much." He paused. "Look, Serena. You're leaving for two weeks. They need a parent to guide them."

A parent to guide them? Serena's blood boiled. "Get out of my sight, Justice, before I say something I'll regret."

Robin took Justice by the arm and led him from the room. "Why don't you wait in the study while Serena thinks things over?" She approached Serena and rubbed her back. "I'll make us a pot of tea. Won't meet tearoom standards, but hopefully it will calm your nerves."

"Thanks, Mama." Serena headed for the banquette, the cozy table with padded benches placed in the kitchen nook. Surrounded by windows on three sides, it gave a wonderful view of her backyard.

Serena gazed out at the New Zealand Christmas tree, her favorite because of the name and the brilliant crimson flowers that burst forth every summer. Being September, the blooms had reached their peak, yet she still saw its beauty.

Robin placed a steaming cup of tea in front of Serena. "Have you had time to think?" She slid onto the bench opposite her daughter.

"No." Serena stared into her cup. "It's not fair, Mama. The girls call Justice and share their news like he's always been there for them. It's not right."

"Sounds like you're a little jealous." Robin stirred her tea. "Serena, you have done an excellent job raising those girls. You made sure they didn't think ill of their dad, even when they only saw him twice a year. Be proud of that fact."

"It's hard," Serena cried.

"They know the difference, baby." Robin reached across the table, and Serena took her mom's hand. "Jade and Jewel are happy to have their dad back in their lives. That's all. They don't intend to create a rivalry between the two of you."

"I rather liked it that way." Serena tried to smile yet failed.

"Show Jade and Jewel what it's like to be magnanimous, sweetie. Generous, you are."

"Okay. But you've got to watch over them, especially Justice, while I'm gone." Serena's phone pinged, and she checked the screen. "It's a message from Jade."

"Go on. Read it."

"Can Jewel and I stay in your suite at The Pearl this weekend? Please. Please. Please. Mrs. Takeda gave the okay," Serena read. She lifted her head to see her mom smiling. "They checked with Nina before contacting me. It was the polite thing to do."

"See," Robin said. "They may have told Justice their plan but needed to go through the right channels before contacting you. Nice work, don't you think?"

"Fine, yes, they followed protocol." Serena typed back a positive message along with heart emojis. "I still need to check with Nina. Does she want Justice there?"

"Serena." Robin folded her hands. "You are the only one with a Justice problem. Nina sees him as the twin's dad. If you don't want him there, she'll abide by your wishes, I'm sure."

"You're saying she doesn't have a problem with Justice. It's just me."

"Well…"

Serena's breath hitched. "I'm alone here, Mama? You're not on my side?"

"I'm always on your side, darling. I have issues with Justice, but you must give him a chance to redeem himself with the girls." Robin sighed. "It's hard, Serena. I'm just as angry at him as you are, but I'm trying to help *you*. You can't see clearly when it comes to your ex-husband."

"You're doing it for me," Serena said in a quiet voice. "I'll call Nina and arrange for Justice to have carte blanche at the hotel."

"I didn't say to go overboard, Sissy." Robin chuckled.

"Sissy. You haven't called me that in a long time, Mama. Have you come to terms with Sasha leaving the family to travel the world?"

"It's been almost twenty years, Serena. She did what she did. My brother was heartbroken and still is."

At thirty-nine, Sasha Robinson, three years younger than Serena, had wanderlust since she could talk. Serena recalled her pointing to pictures of the Taj Mahal, the Eiffel Tower and Niagara Falls saying she wanted to go there. Sasha never chose amusement parks or water parks, like Serena did. She wanted to see the world.

"My cousin always followed her own path, Mama. When Sasha got the offer to study art in Paris, she couldn't turn it down. She had talent. I encouraged her to go. So did you."

"I thought she'd come back, Serena. Not stay there forever." Robin hung her head. "Sasha barely calls or texts her parents or me besides the obligatory holiday and birthday cards."

"Lovingly hand painted and created by her. She makes her living as a watercolorist. Cards, small florals, garden paintings and beautiful landmark images to name a few," Serena replied. "Her life is there. She made a name for herself in Europe, and it has become her career. We need to accept her choice and wish her well. I can't fault Sasha for following her dream, but I wish she'd come home more often."

"More often? She came once for your father's funeral and when your aunt and uncle moved to Nevada."

"That's part of your problem, Mama. You miss your brother," Serena stated. "Uncle Damian and you were close."

"Like you and Sasha," Robin replied. "She was closer to being a sister than a cousin. You called each other Sissy. Once she left, our family fell apart. Dad died, my brother moved to another state, and you divorced Justice."

"Mama, it's not that bad. Plus, Sasha left when she was nineteen. Those other things happened much later. Stop putting the blame on her." Serena rose and joined Robin on her side of the table. She wrapped an arm around the woman's shoulders and laid her head on her mom. "Guess what I learned from all this. Nothing stays the same. I'm sorry your life changed, but I'm happy you're here with me now. We're on a new journey." She kissed her mother's cheek. "Together." Serena reached for her phone. "I'm going to call Nina and tell her Justice will join the girls this weekend."

* * * *

Serena's expansive kitchen seamlessly transitioned into her family room. Choosing the scenic route, she wandered towards the small study near the foyer, from the back of the house. She stopped to admire family pictures along the way. When Serena came upon the photos from the twin's first fashion show, tears welled in her eyes. *Thanks, Mia, for fulfilling their dream.* Taking calming breaths, she realized she had to let go of her anger towards Justice.

Upon her arrival, Serena discovered Justice spinning in the desk chair, rotating one way, then the other. Resting his chin on steepled hands, he appeared to be asleep, yet he couldn't be. His body was moving the seat.

"Justice?"

Startled, Justic looked up and said, "Sorry, you caught me daydreaming. Have you decided?"

"Yes, I'll talk to Nina when I see her tomorrow and tell her you are part of the team."

"Team? I like that."

"Don't like it too much. You can easily be kicked off for any violation."

"And here I thought we made progress." Justice chuckled. "You are still playing the bad cop."

"Not bad, and not a cop, Justice. As a mother bear, I always protect my cubs, no matter how old they are. If you understand that, we're good."

"Oh, I understand." Justice slowly nodded. "Thanks, Serena. I won't disappoint you."

"This is not about me," Serena stated. "Don't disappoint the girls."

Justice rose from the chair and placed his hands on Serena's upper arms. "Hey, baby, I never wanted it to end this way." He leaned in as if to kiss her.

Serena pulled away from his grip and stepped back. "You need to stop pretending that you are attracted to me, Justice. You moved on, and so have I."

"I still find you attractive, Serena." Justice raised his brows. "Is Security Guy going on the book tour?"

"Yes." Serena folded her arms.

Serena would never share her entire schedule with Justice, but Jack planned to stay in New York City on Pearl business, while she continued the tour. She didn't believe Jack's story, yet Serena never asked questions about his actual job at the hotel. One day she hoped he'd confide in her, but their relationship was still new.

"Can he afford to go on his salary?" Justice smirked. "Oh wait, I forgot. Nina is flying you to New York, and your publisher pays for your room."

"Enough." Serena held up her hand. "Quit flaunting the fact you got a substantial raise and promotion at your job."

"I wasn't." The corner of Justice's mouth twitched. "Thanks for remembering. You're impressed, I see."

"I already congratulated you, Justice. After all the years you worked for that tech company, you deserved it."

"Sorry. I guess I wanted to remind you I was a good provider for you and the girls."

"Save the stories for them, Justice. I need to pack. I'll walk you to the door."

"Showing me out?" Justice grinned. "Do I get a goodbye kiss?"

Serena marched Justice to the front door and opened it. She kept him at arms-length, knowing he could catch her off-guard. "I'll tell the girls you'll be at the hotel this weekend," she said. "Enjoy your time with them." She closed the door and leaned against it. "I hope I did the right thing."

"You did," Robin said, giving Serena a start. "I plan to go to the hotel myself this weekend. See what the fuss is all about."

"*Now* I know I did the right thing." Serena embraced her mom and headed up stairs to pack.

Chapter Four

Serena checked out her new hairstyle in the mirror and gave it final approval. She liked to change her hair and appearance often. During the summer, she had worn her straightened hair in a high ponytail and had chosen a braid for the fall. "Easy care for the trip," she told her reflection.

Leaning closer to the mirror, she examined her make-up one more time. The perfect eyeshadow highlighted her brown eyes with flecks of gold. She used the best cream for her face, which kept her honey brown skin smooth and silky. *Not a wrinkle.* She added a touch of blush and more mascara.

"Serena," Robin called. "The limo is here."

"Coming." Serena did a final check of her appearance and scanned her room for forgotten items. Satisfied, she rolled her luggage to the top of the stairs.

The driver stood with her mom at the front door. "Let me get that for you," he said when he spotted her. He bounded up the stairs, grabbed her case and retreated to the first floor.

"Thanks," Serena said when she reached the bottom step. "I guess I have everything." She held out her hands.

"If you forgot something, buy it," Robin replied as she kissed Serena's cheek. "This is so exciting. Book two, Serena. Did you ever think?"

"No. I'm fortunate people noticed my book. Many exceptional stories and authors exist. See you in two weeks, Mama." Serena blew her mom a kiss and followed the driver into the foggy morning. "Karl doesn't seem too bad today," she said, sliding into the back seat. "He may leave before noon."

"Karl?" The driver shut the door and hopped into the driver's seat.

"You never heard of Karl?" Serena asked in a surprised tone.

"I just moved here two months ago," the driver answered.

"Allow me to enlighten you, especially if you intend to live here for a while."

Serena recounted Karl the Fog's tale - the viral sensation of San Francisco - while on the way to The Pearl. Locals had borrowed the name Karl from a well-known movie, which added a touch of whimsy to the pesky fog that greeted people almost daily. In the film, everyone in town was afraid of Karl the giant because they thought he would eat or kill them. Turned out, he was simply hungry and lonely. In San Francisco, that giant was the fog.

The limo pulled up to The Pearl, and after the driver helped Serena from the car, she said, "One more fog fact.

You made it through August, which is the foggiest month. The fog is at its peak in August, so the month is aptly named Fogust."

"I heard that one." The driver laughed, shutting the door. "Text me when you're ready to leave for the airport."

"I will. Thank you." Serena headed into the hotel.

Since Jack resided at The Pearl, they had agreed to meet at the hotel before heading to the airport. This arrangement gave Serena the opportunity to speak with Nina before her departure. Retrieving her phone from her handbag, she sent Nina a text. Once the message sent, she informed Jack of her arrival.

Serena walked into the gardens fully aware Nina would find her. She had said her goodbyes to Samauri, so she avoided the pond. Strolling down the main path, Serena soon heard Nina's voice.

"Serena," she called.

"It was kind of you to meet me," Serena said as Nina approached.

"I rise at five a.m. every day."

"It's six now, and I must be at the airport by seven. A minute is all I need."

"If we run late, I'll call the pilot," Nina said.

"You're too good to me, Nina, but no need to do that. I'll stick to the schedule." Serena took her hand. "Before I go, there's something I need to say. I can't thank you enough for helping my girls." She paused. "Don't let them take advantage of you. I've already spoken with my daughters, but they are still teenagers."

"When have you known someone to take advantage of me?" Nina closed one eye.

"Well…it's just…"

"Serena, I'm teasing. I will set boundaries."

"Do not give them money," Serena responded.

"Only if it helps the hotel," Nina answered. "Deal?"

"Yes. Okay. You win. Again." Serena smiled. "You are family, Nina. A second mother to me. I will always be grateful for your help and guidance. If you ever feel I'm not appreciative or am overstepping, tell me to my face. I can take it."

Nina chuckled. "My dear, dear child. That is why I love you so."

Tears welled in Serena's eyes. "I love you, too."

"Serena?" Jack's voice called to her. "There you are. I imagined you'd be here."

As always, Serena's heart skipped a beat when she saw him. Ruggedly handsome and over six feet tall, Jack had caught her attention last February. *He's everything I wanted in a man. Loyal, kind and fine-looking.* He'd gotten a fresh haircut. His dark hair was short on the sides and longer on the top but less military-style than usual.

Jack's dark brown eyes shone as he came toward her. "Ready?" He turned to Nina. "Good morning, Nina. Thanks for the ride."

"Enjoy." Nina nodded. "I expect a report by the end of the week," she said over her shoulder as she walked down the path.

"A report?" Serena wrinkled her nose.

"Pearl business." Jack smiled.

Although she would love more information, Serena didn't question him. Something else had caught her attention. She pointed to Jack's arm, the one which had suddenly acquired a tattoo. "Is that the…?"

"Dragon?" Jack lifted his sleeve. "You inspired me to get it, Serena. Despite having these dragon symbols for years, this is what I wanted."

"I'm thrilled you got it." Serena tried to recall the dragon's name. "Ree…"

"Ryu, pronounced ree-yooh. The symbols on my other arm stood for dragon. Now I have the real thing." Jack beamed.

"Sorry to use a book analogy, but you've turned the page on your old life, Jack." Serena chuckled. "Get it? Me? I'm an author. Turn the page. Jack, help me out here. You're leaving me dangling here."

"I was enjoying it," Jack replied, lifting the corner of his mouth. "You're right. I'm starting fresh." He took her hand. "With you."

"We have to go, Jack, but first can we…?" Serena stepped close to him, so their bodies touched.

"Kiss?" Jack lightly brushed her lips.

Serena wrapped her arms around his neck and deepened the kiss. Her mind swirled with happiness, knowing Jack had freed himself from his past.

Jack drew back and said, "We'll miss our plane."

"I'll text the driver," Serena replied, slumping her shoulders. Then she remembered and said, "I have you all to myself this week. No interruptions."

"Sounds great." Jack took her hand, and the couple walked to the exit, ready to start their adventure.

* * * *

"What do you mean you booked your own room?" Serena stood in front of her hotel room, key in hand.

"I'm just down the hall," Jack said. "I'm staying longer, remember?"

"Fine. It's fine, Jack." Serena fumbled to open the door. "I'll see you later. Dinner?"

Jack followed Serena into the room. "We need to talk."

Serena spun on her heels. "Is this where you give me the 'It's not you, it's me' speech? Or how about 'Can we just be friends?' I've got more where those came from." She fought back tears. Confused and defeated, Serena could not figure him out. *What does Jack want?*

"Serena." Jack exhaled. "I prefer not to do this here."

"Of course you don't. But you *will* do it here and *now*."

"You've got the wrong idea." Jack stumbled over the words. "Central Park is the more appropriate place. Can you wait?"

"I don't understand, Jack. You better say it before I burst into tears."

"I love you, Serena."

Serena had planned to show Jack to the door before the angry tears started, but he just switched the script. "You what?"

"Love you. I planned to tell you in a romantic setting on this trip. I got the room to prevent any distractions. You have a job to do, and so do I."

Tears rolled down Serena's cheeks, and she swiped them away. "I love you, too, Jack. You don't know how much."

"Whatever you feel, make it times two for me." Jack took Serena in his arms and guided her towards the bed. When he reached the edge, he gently placed her on the comforter. "This is where I want you the most."

"Then stay with me," Serena whispered.

"We will do this the right way," Jack replied. "I'm going to tell you I love you in Central Park as planned, take you to dinner where Mia made reservations for us *then* bring you back here to this bed. You deserve all that, Serena."

"When?"

"When your schedule allows. I'll leave you to unpack and text me when you're ready for dinner."

Serena clung to him before letting him go. "You've made me so happy."

Jack kissed the tip of her nose. "You always make me happy."

* * * *

"It feels like you've been gone forever, Mom," Jewel cried.

"It's only been a week," Serena answered. "How can I assist from long-distance?"

"I'm glad you asked," her daughter replied. "We have a bit of a problem."

"A bit?"

"Yes, tiny."

"Jewel, stop playing and tell me what is happening," Serena huffed.

"Booking well-known artists for the market has not gone well. Most already have other engagements for the holiday season."

"Makes sense. You probably had to contact them a year ago." Serena paced in her hotel room as they spoke. "What about the German guy?"

"He's the only one who has committed. How will that look on a poster? A giant nutcracker with his name next to it." Jewel sounded defeated.

"What about the choir and dancers?"

"Booked. We've had a great response from local talent, and we're conducting a thorough selection process to choose candidates who best meet our standards."

"That sounds promising," Serena said.

"It is, but…"

"Put the phone on speaker, Jewel." Serena heard Jade in the background.

This sounds serious. "Hi, Jade, I wasn't aware you were in the room, too."

"Hi, Mom. What Jewel is attempting to say, and doing a terrible job of it, is could you sign books on opening day and the following two weekends?"

"You would add me to your posters? I'd be a headliner?" Serena teased. "How can I say no?"

"You'll do it?" Jewel asked.

"If it helps your market, of course. But I get to set the times," Serena said.

"Yes, whatever you want," Jade replied. "Where are you, by the way?"

"I'm in Chicago," Serena answered. "From here I fly to Denver."

"How were New York City and Jack?"

"We had a wonderful three days together."

"We love Jack and are glad he's in your life. You sound happy," Jewel said.

"I am. He loves you and Jade, too."

"Mom," Jade said. "One more thing. Can you give us a loan? We promise to pay you back from the money we make at the market."

"So *that's* the real reason you called," Serena replied. "Money. For what?"

"Inventory," Jade answered. "We need to order items ASAP so we can stock our shelves."

"I want to see the list and what you plan to buy," Serena demanded. "Use the emergency credit card."

Serena had provided the girls with a credit card to use only in emergency situations. They never took advantage of that privilege or tried to use it without her permission.

When she presented them with the card, she hoped they'd never feel stranded without aid. It had proved invaluable, especially when Serena wasn't present like now. She could still grant permission to use the card, even from another state.

"Thanks, Mom! You are the best," Jade exclaimed. "We won't keep you. You're busy and probably flying out soon."

"Wait." Serena stopped pacing. "I thought of something. Remember my cousin Sasha? You met her once or twice."

"She lives in Paris, right?" Jewel replied.

"Yes. Sasha is a watercolorist. She is more well-known in Europe than in the states, but if her schedule permits, I'll invite her to participate in the market."

"You would do that?" Jade asked in a high-pitched voice.

"Of course, but don't get your hopes up until I speak with her," Serena said. "We could even have family Christmas together. Something we haven't done in years. Grandma and Uncle Damian would love it."

"Please try to make it work, Mom," Jewel begged. "I just looked her up on my phone. Her paintings are beautiful."

Serena swallowed. Could she convince her cousin to fly to the states for an unproven Christmas market? Let alone stay and celebrate the holidays with family? She once knew her cousin well, but a few texts and short phone calls over the years hadn't kept their close friendship intact. *What if she's changed?* "I'm sure she'll come, girls," Serena said. "Don't worry."

Chapter Five

"Serena, I am *so* busy that time of year," Sasha said, after hearing Serena's proposal. "It's the reason I don't come home for Christmas."

"Let's get real, Sasha. You use that excuse every year. What's the actual reason you don't want to come home?"

"My parents are overbearing, Serena," Sasha replied, letting out a breath. "If they had their say, I'd be their next-door neighbor forever. You're an only child like me. You understand."

"No. I do not. My parents were fine."

"You always complained about them needing to know your location and how long you'd be away," Sasha said.

"We were teenagers," Serena stated. "Give me another reason you don't come home. Make it a good one."

"Rory."

"Rory Harris? Your high school boyfriend?"

"We had a bad break-up, Serena. It sounds silly, but I wish I had talked him into coming to Paris. He's married with two kids now."

"So? You won't run into him. Your parents don't live in San Francisco anymore. They moved to Vegas." Serena exhaled. "I think you are inventing excuses. Why don't you say you're too lazy to book a flight? Or you get claustrophobia on the plane? What about jet lag?"

"This isn't funny, but you're making me laugh," Sasha said with a chuckle. "Truthfully? I don't come home because I'm a disappointment to my parents. I never married or had kids."

"They just want to see *you*, Sasha. And you are *not* a disappointment. You're a successful artist and entrepreneur."

"You haven't seen the expressions on my parents' faces when they ask if I've met anyone. They're desperate for grandchildren."

"You live in Paris, and your parents would never see them," Serena said. "When do all these parental looks happen? You're never here."

"It's the twenty-first century, Sis. We video chat." Sasha paused. "I'll tell you what. If I send you everything I need for my sales booth, and you do all the work, I will take part in the girls' market. Also, a hotel suite. I'm not staying with you or Aunt Robin."

"My mom lives with me now, Sasha," Serena replied.

"Oh my, how did *that* happen? You'll have to fill me in on the details when I arrive." Sasha laughed.

"I'll send you a more complete schedule of the event when we have it," Serena said, ignoring Sasha's comment. "Thanks for doing this. It will be great to see you."

* * * *

After a whirlwind second week, the book tour ended, and Serena found herself walking into The Pearl Hotel. Happy to be home, she headed straight for the tearoom, eager to catch up with friends.

"Serena!" Mia rose to greet her. "Tell us everything."

"I only want to know what happened with Jack," Lily said, waiting for a hug. "Start talking."

"Jack is wonderful," Serena replied, taking her seat. "Ooh, I see you ordered my tea."

"We did." Mia smiled. "Now, as they say, spill the tea."

Serena poured the steaming amber liquid into the cup with precision. "We had three romantic days together. That's all I'm saying."

"Did you finally…" Lily twirled her finger in the air.

"A woman does not kiss and tell," Serena answered.

"You did!" Lily lightly clapped her hands. "I am so happy for you."

"We won't ask a thing, Serena," Mia said, glancing at her from the corner of her eye. "Unless you wish you share."

"It's your turn to share." Serena stared at Mia, then turned to Lily. "Have you been helping the girls or are you letting them make their own mistakes?"

"Both." Lily smiled. "They are smart, ambitious girls, Serena. It's almost October, and their plan is in place."

"Lucky for them, we have weddings at The Pearl," Mia said. "I introduced them to Randi, our event coordinator, and she took them on a tour of the storage room. We have many types of lighted trees, snow-covered bridges, and enough props to help them decorate the gardens for the holidays."

"I must thank Randi personally," Serena replied. She had worked with the woman on several occasions and always found her helpful.

"Randi asked to be included on their design team. Everyone is excited." Mia took a sip of tea. "Jade and Jewel want to introduce us to some of the local talent, too. This weekend, the girls will show the facilities to the vendors and entertainers."

"I missed a lot." Serena winced. "I'm sorry you had to shoulder the burden."

"It wasn't a burden. We're having fun. Right, Lily?" Mia faced her.

"Mia's right." Lily nodded. "We are having a blast. Honestly, I had doubts, but the girls' work ethic impresses me. Justice has dedicated his fair share of time and effort, too."

"Justice?" Serena bit her lip. *Don't say a word.*

"Nina gave him a spot in the storage room to set up shop. She brought in a table saw and other tools he needed. He's built the girls a cute, framed house with an open front. They're painting it now."

"I'd love to see it," Serena said. "Plus, I have more work for him." She told her friends about her cousin Sasha. "Sasha will come if all goes well. The holiday season is busy for her. Besides painting, she owns a little shop in Paris."

"I love her work," Mia gushed. "I had no idea she was your cousin, Serena. Why didn't you tell us?"

"You're familiar with her paintings?" Serena raised her brows. "She'll be happy to hear."

"Yes, her talent is unbelievable. I'd love to design her booth," Mia said. "The girls decided sellers should have booths that resemble quaint little shops. They've brought in artists from their school to help with the painting. Sasha should have a holiday-themed Parisian storefront. Won't it be cute?"

"Sasha would love it," Serena answered. "She'll also be thrilled that you created her shop." Her heart fluttered with excitement. *This could potentially work out and become a success.*

"I'd love to see what's going on in the storage room. Does anyone know if Justice is here?" Serena checked her watch. "Never mind. It's five o'clock. He's still at work." She pushed back her chair. "I'm going to take a quick peek."

"What they've accomplished will impress you," Mia said. "Enjoy."

"Talk later." Lily waved as Serena headed for the tearoom exit.

* * * *

Serena peeked into the event coordinator's office. "Randi?"

"Serena! Good to see you." Randi rose from her chair. "Come in."

"I came to thank you for helping my girls."

"No need. I loved every minute." Randi rounded her desk and perched on its corner. She motioned to the sofa across from it. "Please, sit."

"I'd love to, but I can't stay. I came to ask a favor."

"Ask away."

"Is the storage room open or locked?" Serena asked.

"Locked, but I give keys to those who need access."

Serena closed one eye. "Like Justice?"

"Yes." Randi laughed. "Like Justice."

"Is he there now?"

"I don't believe so. Let's walk over, and I'll open the door. When you leave, just make sure it locks behind you."

"Thanks for doing this," Serena said.

The hallway leading to the reception and bridal rooms included offices for the event staff. Upon reaching the end, Randi stood in front of a door Serena hadn't noticed before.

"This is it," Randi said as she tapped on the wood. "Don't underestimate what's behind this door. It *will* surprise you. It's much bigger inside than you would think."

"Like the Tardis?" Serena joked.

Randi gave her a strange look.

"The sci-fi show? You know, it's bigger on the inside than it looks from the outside…" Serena waved her hand. "Never mind."

Randi unlocked and pushed back the door. She stepped aside to let Serena go first.

Serena's jaw dropped as she took in the three-story-high structure. "It's as big as a football field." She glanced up at the skylights. "With natural lighting, too."

"It's not as big as a football field, but close." Randi chuckled. "We have plenty of space. Come on. I'll show you the work area for the Christmas market."

The concrete floors and metal shelving reminded Serena of being in a big-box home-improvement store, only much nicer. The room's center provided ample space for working on displays. Two forklifts parked in one corner caught her attention. "This is unbelievable."

Serena followed Randi to an open area in the far-left section. "We have workspaces throughout the room. We need them since we have many projects going on at once," Randi said. "I assigned this one to the market." She pointed toward the farthest corner, and Serena spotted the table saw Nina had provided, plus lumber and half-built projects. "That's Justice's area."

Searching for the girls' shop, Serena recognized the almost-finished product and rushed to see it closer. "This is Jade and Jewel's shop. Am I right?"

"Yes." Randi smiled.

"Oh, my. It's beautiful."

"Let me tell you what is great about these shops," Randi replied. "Justice built them in a way that makes it easy to take them apart to move or store them."

"He always had the skill," Serena said. She stepped back to admire the twins' work.

The exterior of the wooden structure wore a sandy color hue accented with mocha trim. Inside, a deep sky blue adorned the walls, which Serena felt would complement the merchandise. She admired the evergreen wreath entwined with scarlet ribbon painted on the back wall. Dark green holly encircled the three interior walls, and someone had cleverly tied white snowflakes to the border. Painted presents in various shapes, sizes, and colors adorned the bottom of the back wall.

Randi handed Serena a key. "Come anytime you'd like. I must return to the office, but you're welcome to stay as long as you wish."

"Thanks, Randi." Serena walked around the structure, checking for any missed spots or mistakes. "Well done," she said under her breath.

Returning to the open front of the shop, Serena stepped inside and said, "All it needs is shelves to display their products."

"I plan to work on shelves tonight," a voice said from behind her.

Justice's voice startled Serena, and she placed her hand on her heart. Turning to face him, she hissed, "Don't sneak up on me like that, Justice Tate."

"Sorry. You had your back turned, Serena. I didn't see you until I had reached the work area." Justice stuck out his lower lip. "Forgive me?"

"No." Serena pushed past him. "I was just leaving."

"Didn't look like it to me."

"Fine. I *wasn't* leaving. I wanted to find something I could do to help."

"You could hold the shelf brackets while I screw them into the wall."

"I can do that." Serena held out her hand. "Give me one and tell me where to place it."

"I've already marked the walls. Jewel and Jade have painted the shelves so we can place them on the brackets once we finish."

Serena and Justice worked silently until one wall was complete. She took a breath and said, "I have a favor to ask."

Justice raised his brows. "Oh, really? Do tell."

"Do you remember my cousin Sasha?"

"Vaguely. Is she the one who moved to Paris twenty years ago?"

"Yes, my only cousin on my mom's side of the family." Serena told Justice about her conversation with Sasha, succinctly as she could. "Would you be willing to build her shop?"

"I'm doing most of them now, Serena. What's one more?" Justice shrugged.

"Thank you!" Serena was about to fling her arms around him yet held herself back. "I appreciate the gesture. How will you finish everything by opening day?"

"You should see this place on weekends." Justice whistled. "The vendors come and do what they can. Each oversees their own shop. Some have brought family who are proficient in building or working with wood."

"Wow. I had no idea." Serena shook her head.

"Neither did I." Justice ran his hand over the top of his head. "It's nice being part of something this big."

"It is big, isn't it?" Serena laughed.

"There you are." Jack's voice traveled toward her.

"Jack?" Serena waved. "You're back."

"Hey, that rhymes," Justice said under his breath, inching closer.

"Stop." Serena elbowed him in case he had any ideas, like putting his arm around her or kissing her in front of Jack to make him jealous.

Jack was almost to the workshop, and Serena rushed into his arms. "I missed you," she said, kissing him. "Come and see the twins' store."

"Need help?" Jack asked, nodding at Justice.

"We were putting up brackets," Serena answered. "Why don't you take my job, and I'll put the shelves on the finished wall." She faced Justice. "Where are they?"

"Over there." Justice gestured to a tall, wide shelf against the wall. He seemed displeased with the change, but Serena knew she had made the right decision.

Serena searched through the smooth, white shelving until she found the lengths she needed to place atop the brackets. One by one, she carried and placed them in their correct spots. Once she finished, she stepped back and admired her work. "It looks wonderful, better than I could have imagined."

"If all shops have this shape," Jack said. "You can easily design Sasha's shop."

"You know about Sasha?" Justice asked.

"Of course he does, Justice. Jack is my boyfriend." Serena glanced at Jack, giving him a loving look. "A boyfriend who is taking me to dinner right now."

"I already made the reservation," Jack said, and offered Serena his arm. "Great work, Justice. Happy to help any time."

Chapter Six

"Red and silver will be the primary colors of the market." Jade linked arms with Serena as she and her daughters walked through the gardens. "The landscape team will place artificial snow in the beds along with those bare-branch white trees with lights. We'll place peppermint candies mounted on poles along the edges. It's just a start. We have more ideas."

"You're off to an excellent start, Jade." Serena patted her hand.

"We'll place those shiny silver trees on either side of the benches throughout the gardens," Jewel said. "They won't have lights or ornaments because they can reflect light and make their own show."

"Samurai will like that," Serena replied.

"Your fish?" Jewel wrinkled her nose. "Despite the time I've spent in the gardens and by the pond, I still haven't seen a red and white koi."

"He's there." Serena defended the koi. "Trust me."

"Mia thinks he's your imaginary friend." Jade laughed.

"Does she now? When did she say that?" Serena stopped walking and stared at the girls.

"She was joking, Mom. Mia would never make fun of you," Jewel said. "We mentioned we never saw Samurai when we met by the pond to discuss décor."

"Jewel!" a tall, slender, yet muscular young man called from a distance. His layered brown hair skimmed along his shoulders as he jogged toward them.

"Carmody!" Jewel rushed up to him and took his hand. "Come and meet my mom."

"Ms. Tate." Carmody bowed his head. "It is a pleasure to be in such great company."

Girls were right. He's a little over the top. "Hello, Carmody. Are you here to rehearse?"

"Not today. Jewel invited me to..." Carmody gave her daughter a sweet smile, and Jewel returned it.

"Meet me here." Jewel finished his thought.

He likes her! She likes him! How did I miss that? Serena attempted to make eye contact with Jade, but her other daughter had turned away. "That is kind of you, Carmody," Serena said, not knowing how to react. *Why did I just say that?*

"Carm also has a fitting with Mia," Jewel replied. "She offered to make him a new elf costume. His was..."

"Lacking." Carmody laughed, and Jewel joined in as she hooked her arm through his.

Speechless, Serena walked to where Jade stood, taking photos. "Jade!" she said in a stage whisper. "Why didn't you tell me that Carmody..."

"Is white?" Jade teased.

"No. Stop that. Are Carmody and Jewel dating?"

"Almost."

"What kind of answer is 'almost'?"

"They're in the 'getting to know you' phase. Sort of like you and Jack."

"Don't compare our relationships. And besides, Jack and I are a couple."

"It's official?" Jade widened her eyes. "Congrats."

"What are you congratulating Mom for?" Jewel asked, joining the group.

"Mom and Jack finally did the deed," Jade answered, jabbing Serena in her ribs with an elbow.

"I did not say that, young lady." Serena placed her hand on her hip.

"You inferred it, Mom. She used the word 'couple', Jewel, when referring to her and Jack. Something she's never said before." Jade giggled and waved her index finger at Serena. "Mom! You always do that to distract us."

"Do what?"

"Your pose. The hand on your hip. Like you mean business."

Serena wanted to change the subject, so she glanced over her shoulder. "You better get back to Carmody, Jewel. He looks lost."

"He's not, Mom," Jewel replied, but headed toward him.

"Any more surprises, Jade?" Serena asked. "Anything you want to tell me?'

"I do not have a boyfriend, if that's what you're asking. I am single and like it that way."

"But you would tell me, right?" Serena cringed.

"Yes, I would. Now, would you like to meet the Austrian choir? They want to practice on the stage Dad built in the wedding chapel. They should be here soon."

* * * *

"Staged events will happen here," Jade said to Serena, gesturing to the two-level stage which filled the wedding canopy. The staff had secured the silky white fabric to the poles, easy to untie if walls were required. "When the time comes, it will be fun to decorate this area."

"Excuse me, Jade, but Jewel said we'd find you here." A male voice tinged with an Austrian accent made Serena pivot on her heels.

"Oh, hello." Serena nodded.

"You must be Jade and Jewel's mother."

"I am."

"Mom." Jade stepped between them. "This is Mr. Gruber, the choir director."

"Jade." Mr. Gruber made a noise in his throat. "I keep telling you to call me Max."

"Okay. Max, this is my mom, Serena Tate."

"I am well acquainted with your books." Max took Serena's hand in his, and she prayed he didn't kiss the top.

Max Gruber sported a dark blonde mustache with touches of gray. It matched his full head of hair and brows. His blue eyes had a mischievous twinkle, yet Serena had learned not to make hasty judgments. She'd remain neutral until she learned more about him.

"I have brought my best singers today." Max swept his hand to the young adults who stood behind him. "These talented individuals will create beautiful music at the market. Thank you for inviting us." He pointed to a young man with reddish-blonde hair. "Felix, if you would please begin."

Felix stepped forward and said, "I am Felix Kulmer. A junior at the university."

After he finished, a girl joined him. "I am Marie Theyer. Sophomore at the university."

"Oh, I get it. They're acting like those kids in that musical. Do, re, mi…" Serena swallowed her laugh when Max looked at her as if she interrupted an important moment. Maybe he was stricter than she initially believed.

Two girls stepped into the front line. "I am Anna Wagner, a junior at the university, and this is my sister, Sophie. She's a freshman."

Alexander, Alex for short, introduced himself, followed by Leo. Both announced they attended the university and were sophomores.

Serena tried to memorize the members' names but finally gave up. She smiled at the choir and said, "It's nice to meet you. I can't wait to hear you sing."

"Feel free to practice and test the stage," Jade said. She took her mom's hand. "I just got a text from Sunita. She and her dance group are at the Torii gate."

"Jade, so very nice to see you." Sunita smiled when Serena and Jade reached the garden's entrance. She gestured to the people trailing behind her. "I've brought my dancers and musicians today. We'd love to rehearse, if possible."

"The Vienna choir group is in the staging area, Sunita," Jade answered. "Max has a half hour to make preliminary plans and adjustments. After that, it's your turn. Please, enjoy the gardens while you wait."

"I will set a timer." Sunita smiled and tapped her wrist. She turned to the students. "Everyone, follow me."

"Come on, Mom. More people to meet. They're in the storage room, working on their shops."

After entering the storage area, Serena took in the sights and sounds of individuals working on their craft. Artists had created pottery, wall hangings, and sculptures to fill their shops. She admired a photography booth decorated with vintage cameras. The student had plans to sell photos and take pictures of guests against a Christmas backdrop painted on the shop's back wall for a nominal fee.

Jade led her toward a cute shop designed like a bakery. "This is my favorite," she said. "Natasha plans to sell gingerbread men and build-your-own gingerbread house kits besides Christmas cookies. Another bakery is selling cakes and pies."

When they completed the tour, Serena remarked, "You've thought of everything, Jade. Well done. The market offers food, drink, toys, holiday decorations and gift ideas."

"Thanks. I think it will be great."

"But it's quite a cast of characters you have assembled, Jade. I hope everyone will get along."

"How can they not?" Jade lifted her hands in the air, showing her palms. "Everyone will be in the holiday spirit."

* * * *

Mother and daughter walked to the back entrance of the indoor gardens. They followed the path which led past a shrine. Decorative before Nina's brother had died, it now held Kaito's ashes. "Hey, Kaito." Serena waved as she passed by.

"Do you always greet Mrs. Takeda's brother?" Jade asked.

"Always." Serena smiled.

"From now on, I will, too." Jade stopped to admire the shrine. She turned to Serena and said, "Am I hearing things or do you hear yelling?"

"I believe I do." Serena grabbed her daughter's hand. "Let's go."

Following the sound, Serena and Jade wound up at the garden wedding chapel. Max Gruber stood towering over Sunita, his face turning a deep shade of red. "I had another five minutes, Ms.…?"

"Patel." Sunita fisted her hands and placed them on her hips. Her black braid swung from one side to the other as she shook her head.

"You have now wasted that number of minutes with your silly argument," Max chided. He faced his singers.

"You are free to go. Next practice is Sunday night. Seven o'clock. Do not be late."

"I'll bring snacks," Anna announced as the group dispersed.

"I'm in charge of drinks," Leo shouted.

Serena thought the students appeared happy to leave or perhaps they were just cheerful in general. She didn't know which to believe. *They signed up for choir. It's not mandatory, so it must be fun.*

Max pushed past Jade and Serena as if he hadn't noticed them. Serena widened her eyes as she turned to Jade. "Does he have a temper?"

"Not that I'm aware." Jade shrugged. "He is a perfectionist though." She turned to Sunita. "I am sorry. I should have been here."

"Do not worry, dear." Sunita took Jade's hand. "Mr. Gruber is a cantankerous old man."

"You know him?" Serena asked.

"Yes, we both work at the university. He is head of the music department."

"Is that the reason he left Austria?" Serena asked. "The university offered him a job?"

"I believe so. People say he has demons hidden in his closet." Sunita lifted her shoulder. "Let's not speak of him again. I have an idea. What if my troupe dances in open spaces, Jade? You can still schedule us for a show on the stage, but we can perform one dance anywhere in the gardens."

"Jade?" Serena made eye contact with her daughter. "She makes a good point."

"Okay," Jade answered. "One show on the stage and one dance every half hour throughout the gardens. I need to record this in my notes and create a schedule. Where is Jewel? She needs to hear this."

Serena noticed Jewel and Carmody speaking with the choir at the hotel's entrance. "I'll get her."

As she neared the students, Serena noticed an uneasy vibe between Carmody and Felix. The expression on their faces showed their mutual dislike. Before she reached the group, Felix pushed Carmody in the chest and she heard him say, "Back off, Carm. You don't need to be in everyone's business."

"He's not," Jewel defended him. "Carm wants to make the market a success. You could try being helpful and answer his questions."

"Hello, everyone," Serena said, a little too brightly. "Jewel." She faced her daughter. "Jade is making major decisions without you. I think you should join her."

"I'm leaving now, Jewel," Carmody said. He squeezed her upper arm. "We'll talk later."

Serena waited until Carmody and the choir left the hotel before she said, "Why did you leave your sister, Jewel? She's working hard, and you're hanging out with friends."

"I wasn't, Mom. Since Carm won't have a booth, we were scoping out places he could use as a base."

"Did you find one?" Serena asked.

"Several."

As they drew closer to Jade, Serena wanted to quiz her daughter before they arrived. "Is something going on between Felix and Carmody?"

"No." Jewel hung her head.

"That sounded like a yes." Serena stopped and took Jewel's hand. "You can tell me, baby."

"Felix liked me, Mom," Jewel said in almost a whisper. "No, I should say he *likes* me. He's jealous of Carm."

Serena raised her brows. "So he uses bodily harm to get even?"

"They weren't fighting, Mom. It was just a push," Jewel replied.

"Which could turn into something else. I don't want you involved in a physical altercation."

"It won't come to that." Jewel let go of Serena's hand. "Carm wanted Felix's opinion on his elf character. He asked if he could dance around the choir when they sing."

"I bet that went well," Serena said under her breath.

"Felix said, 'Get out of my face,' to Carm and pushed him."

"I don't like it, Jewel." Serena pressed her lips together and shook her head.

"Like what?" Justice walked toward Serena and Jewel.

"Where did you pop out from?" Serena asked, touching her throat.

"I'm always here on Saturdays, Serena. Why are you surprised?" Justice stared at her.

Serena remembered her promise. Justice could help the girls, and she would play nice. "I'm not. Jewel and I were having a private conservation, and you seemed to jump out of the bushes. Hypothetically, that is."

"Is this serious?" Justice pointed at Serena, then Jewel.

Jewel gave Serena a 'please don't tell him' look. "Mom and I were talking about one of the shops. It's not up to standards. I must tactfully ask Maggie Potts to repaint her shop. How do I go about it?"

"The pie and cake woman?" Justice cringed. "Good luck. I don't have an answer."

"What about Maggie Potts?" Serena asked, her nerves jangling. "Does she have a problem?"

"Everything must be her way or the highway," Justice said with a humorless laugh. "I'm with you, Jewel. Her design is boring. It needs to scream pies and cakes for the holidays."

"I have an idea, Justice," Serena said. "It sounds like you're the man for the job. You get to tell Maggie that her shop needs repainting." She turned to Jewel. "Don't you think so?"

Jewel blinked and bit her lip as if to stop herself from laughing. "I wholeheartedly agree," she said.

"Hey, you two are ganging up on me." Justice held his hands in the air as if surrendering. "Let me see what I can do."

Chapter Seven

Since she lived close to the airport, Serena had agreed to collect her cousin and transport her to the hotel. "Just like my good old rideshare days," Serena mumbled. She waited in the designated area until she received Sasha's call.

"Serena," Sasha said in a breathless tone. "I'm here. I can't believe I'm home."

"I'll be at baggage claim in a few minutes," Serena replied. She started the car and followed the signs until she reached the correct airline.

Sasha stood on the curb, appearing young and fit, examining each car that passed her with a concerned expression. Serena pulled over and parked, then hopped from the driver's seat. "Sasha!" She waved her hand over her head.

"Serena!" Sasha rolled her luggage along the pavement. "You look wonderful," she said as they embraced. "The same Serena I remember."

"You, too." Serena squeezed and released her. "We better get going before we're told to move along."

Once in the car, Serena studied her cousin's appearance. Not much had changed, except her hair. Sasha wore it parted to one side, and the straight shiny locks ended at her chin. *Makeup is flawless. I'll have to quiz her on brands.*

Sasha's chestnut brown eyes glimmered with tears, which Serena hoped were happy ones. She offered her hand. "Are you glad to be home?"

"Yes." Sasha nodded. "I didn't mean to cry."

"You're not. You're happy."

"I believe I am. Funny how it takes years to come to terms with life." Sasha smiled at Serena. "Even though there are miles between us, I hope I've been a good friend."

"You are," Serena answered. "Despite living across the pond, as they say."

"And the time difference." Sasha chuckled. She pointed at Serena. "You got all my shipments?"

"We did. The girls enjoyed unpacking the boxes and said it was like opening Christmas gifts. One surprise after another. Your shop is ready to go, painted with a Parisian Christmas theme by my friend, Mia Takeda."

"I love her!" Sasha exclaimed. "I can't wait to see."

"Since you waited until the last minute, you'll see the completed project." Serena tried not to sound as if she was scolding her cousin, but Sasha did arrive at the last minute. "Tonight, we set up the displays, and tomorrow we'll stock the shelves and have dress rehearsal."

"I couldn't get away until now. Sorry." Serena slumped into her seat. "I hope my associates can cover the holiday rush while I'm gone. It's already been super busy."

"They'll manage. Besides, you're a phone call away." Serena pulled into The Pearl's driveway. "Try to enjoy the time here. Everyone can't wait to meet you."

"I'm excited to meet your fashion designer friend, Mia Takeda. Will her partner, Jordan, be here?"

"Not today," Serena replied.

Upon entering the hotel, Jade and Jewel were the first to welcome them. "Auntie Sasha, we're so happy to see you," Jewel said, rushing toward her, arms opened for a hug.

"We can't wait to show you around," Jade said, joining Jewel in the embrace.

"What about me?" Serena asked. "Do I get a hug?"

"Mom." Jade closed one eye. "You're kidding, right? We saw you this morning."

Lily and Mia stood quietly in the background, and Serena motioned to them. "Sasha," she said. "I want you to meet my friends, Lily Nichols and Mia Takeda Phillips."

Everyone seemed to speak at once, and Serena held up her hand. "Let me get Sasha settled in her room, and we'll return for the grand tour ending at the tearoom."

""I'd like to give her a private tour of the storage room," Justice said, emerging from the gardens.

"Hmm, that sounds a little naughty, Justice." Sasha fluttered her lashes. "It's good to see you. The last time was at…"

"A funeral?" Justice wrinkled his nose.

"Ooh, let's not reminisce then," Sasha said in a playful voice.

Is she flirting with Justice? I assumed there was a code for that. Friends don't date friend's exes. Does that apply to family? And what about the funeral? The only funeral she came home for was my dad's. How can she joke about that?

"Mom," Jewel whispered. "Why do you look like you smelled something bad?"

"I didn't. I don't. I…" Serena shook her head. "Never mind. I'm going to the front desk to get Sasha's room number and key."

When Serena returned, Justice had gone, and the women stood in a group, talking and laughing like old friends.

"Mom." Jewel motioned to her. "Jade and I want to discuss something before you take Aunt Sasha upstairs." They stepped away from the other women. "It's about Josef Bauer, the German Nutcracker King."

Surprised by the news, Serena asked, "Are you certain he wants to be called the German Nutcracker King?"

"Yes," Jade answered, rolling her eyes. "He's quite demanding. Josef insisted Lily change the font on the advertising poster…twice. He also wanted to mount two six-foot-high flat wooden nutcrackers to the Torii gate. One on each side."

Serena gasped. "What did Nina say? You informed her of his request, right?"

"We asked," Jewel assured her. "Mrs. Takeda said if they stood in front of the pillars, it would be alright. No attaching anything to the gate."

"Oh, my." Serena touched her cheek. "He's only been here two days and is already causing trouble."

"Plus." Jade held up her pointer finger. "Josef insisted we place his shop in the most trafficked area." She gestured to the main walkway, which split into various paths. "Right by the pond."

"Why are you giving in to his demands?" Serena asked.

"He's our main attraction, Mom, *and* he came from Germany to participate in the show."

"Okay. Let me think." Serena tapped her chin. "If he continues to be a diva, I'll speak with him."

"You will?" Jewel smiled. "We'd appreciate it. Oh, there's one more thing."

"What?" Serena's head began to hurt.

"When you meet Josef Bauer, don't be surprised by his outfit. The only thing we've seen him wear is the traditional German costume with Lederhosen."

"Those leather trousers ending just above the knee?" Serena wrinkled her nose.

"Yes." Jewel nodded. "With suspenders over a white shirt."

"You left out the best part, Jewel," Jade said. "He always wears a hat. It's green with a rounded front and has a feather attached to the side, like Peter Pan." She giggled. "It's called an Alpine hat. I looked it up."

"Wow. Okay. He's playing the part," Serena said. "Let me take care of my cousin, and we'll attack this later. When does Nina plan to close the gardens?"

"Tonight, after the restaurants close. It will be a long night," Jade responded.

"Are you staying at the hotel?" Serena asked.

"We already put our stuff in your room, Mom," Jewel replied.

"Good." Serena turned to her cousin. "Come on, Sasha. I'll take you to your room."

"We'll wait here," Jade said. "Don't take too long. I want to hear all about Paris."

"Serena," Sasha said, when they walked into the elevator hallway. "Your girls are beautiful. Pictures don't do them justice." She chuckled. "Did I say justice?"

Serena narrowed her eyes. "You did."

"Hey." Sasha placed her hand on Serena's arm. "I'd never go after your man."

"He's not *my* man but thank you. I'm glad to hear you have boundaries."

"I certainly do." Sasha folded her arms. "When do I meet this new man in your life?"

"Maybe tonight, but definitely tomorrow. He has put in a lot of hours helping the girls turn their dream into a reality."

"Sounds like my kind of man," Sasha purred.

That meant nothing. Harmless fun. Serena entered the elevator and pressed the button for the correct floor. "Jack is wonderful," she said and remained silent for the rest of the ride.

* * * *

When Serena and Sasha returned to the gardens, Jade skipped up to her and said, "Mom, Mrs. Takeda gave us a wonderful idea." She linked arms with Serena. "You can be our human resource director."

"Nina suggested this?" Serena stared at her daughter.

"We asked her thoughts on sending individuals to you for help with their issues. She recommended the title."

"I'm trying to stay in the background, Jade, and let you and your sister do your thing. You're in charge."

"We're already overwhelmed with tasks and have so much to do. Please?" Jade begged.

"I would be the complaint department," Serena said. She folded her arms to think it over.

"You're so good with people, Mom, plus you have experience. That's what you always told us, right? You felt like a therapist on your rideshare job." Jade gave her a puppy dog look which would melt anyone's heart. "Please?"

"Since you asked so nicely…okay. Where is my office?" Serena checked the surrounding area.

"You're going to love this part. The tearoom. Mrs. Takeda suggested the location and will provide a workspace for you. Tonight, during setup, everyone will receive a pamphlet containing market rules and regulations."

"If my first guess is correct, my name as human resource director is already in there," Serena replied.

"Mom, look. It's Jack." Jade left her side to greet him.

"Saved by the bell," Serena mumbled.

Serena smiled as Jewel also joined Jack and her sister. They appeared to be in a deep discussion when Sasha approached her. "Is that him?" she asked. "Your guy?"

"Yes, it's Jack."

"Again, you did not do him justice." Sasha covered her mouth. "There I go again. I can't stop saying that word."

"I'll forgive you one more time, then you must choose another," Serena smirked. "Let me introduce you."

Jack was his gallant self, and Serena's heart flipped as always when he made small gestures known only to her. He volunteered to assist Sasha with her shop until she gave final approval. "Tonight, we'll construct the village, and tomorrow is for product placement," he informed the women. "Also, Serena, Jewel told me that we may have to reign in a rowdy group of gingerbread people once they arrive." He chuckled.

Serena found a moment to pull Jack aside from her cousin and daughters. "Did you know about my job?" she asked.

"Human resource director?" Jack raised his brows. "Yeah. I'll help whenever I can."

"Thanks." Serena dropped her voice and glanced at Sasha and her girls. "Do you feel my cousin is flirting with you or is it my imagination?"

"I haven't noticed." Jack took Serena by the shoulders. "I only have eyes for you."

Serena faced him and said, "Ahh, you're sweet, but answer the question."

"Okay, yes." Jack kissed her cheek. "Let me ask you something. Even though you've barely seen her in the past twenty years, did she always behave like that? Maybe it's just her way, and you forgot."

"You could be right." Serena shook her head. "I can't remember. We flirted with guys back in the day, then I was with Justice…" Serena paused. "Never mind. I'm overthinking things."

"There you are!" A booming voice cut into their conversation.

"Josef." Jack nodded his head. "Have you met Serena Tate, the girls' mother?"

"I have not had the honor," Josef said in a thick German accent. "It is a pleasure." He cleared his throat. "I read the flyer. I'll come to you when I have a problem."

The man reminded Serena of a huge black bear, but cinnamon in color. His beard spilled onto his barrel chest, and she could barely see his mouth through all the hair. He wore the exact attire the girls had described: black Lederhosen, a white shirt with black suspenders bearing a floral design and a green Alpine hat.

"I hope you don't have a problem yet," Serena said, trying to give him her best smile.

"Och, no. But if I do, you will be my first stop." Josef shook his pointer finger at her and chuckled. "Jack." He clapped his hand over Jack's shoulder. "I am ready for duty. Text when ready."

"Whoa," Serena whispered as the man walked away. "I didn't expect that. I had pictured him differently."

"As one of Santa's little helpers working furiously on his nutcrackers?" Jack teased.

"Something like that." Serena shook her head. "I'm overwhelmed and need a break."

"A cup of tea might help," Jack said. "I'll escort you to the tearoom, then head down to the security offices. I must ensure all cameras are functional for the event."

When the group arrived at the tearoom, Serena found Nina standing in the doorway. "Serena, my dear. Introduce me to your cousin." After the niceties were over, she said, "Girls, would you please take Sasha to our table? I need to speak with your mother."

Serena's heart pounded. *This seems serious. Has Nina discovered a problem?* "Okay, they're gone. Let me have it." She held her breath.

"I want to show you the location of the human resource office," Nina said, sweeping her hand towards a large table close to the entrance. "The hostess can easily send people your way. You will also have a sign on the table. Do you approve?"

"That's it?" Serena exhaled. "Nothing ominous has happened? Wait a minute. Has there been an underlying threat?" She widened her eyes.

Nina chuckled. "You have quite the creative imagination, Serena, which helps your writing. But no, nothing close to that. I don't foresee anything unusual happening, just the minor problems which can arise at any event and the reason I want you here. But." Nina pressed her lips together.

"I *knew* there was a 'but'."

"You never know," Nina said in a quieter voice. "You are the best person for the job, no matter what happens. Now, let's go join the others."

Chapter Eight

Serena let the twins have her room while she slept on the sofa bed. They'd called it quits at three a.m. and dragged themselves up to her suite, tired but happy with the results. Her alarm rang at seven, startling Serena awake. She heard the shower, signaling someone had already started their day. She stretched, rolled to the mattress edge, and stared at the wall.

"Hi, Mom," Jade said in a perky voice.

"Hello, sweetie. I think I'm getting old. I need a gallon of coffee to start the day."

"The tearoom is setting up a buffet for the workers," Jade answered. "I'm sure they'll have coffee." She paused. "Won't they be disappointed when you refuse to drink tea?"

"Not today, they won't." Serena chuckled.

"I'm going down. See you later." Jade waved as she headed for the door.

"Hey, wait for me," Jewel shouted from the bedroom. She rushed past Serena, blew a kiss and nodded at her sister, who held back the door.

"I guess I'm next." Serena slid her feet into her slippers and shuffled to the bathroom.

Serena, having showered and donned a t-shirt and jeans, felt prepared for the day. She enjoyed the quiet time, and it had given her time to think. *When I see the girls, I must address this issue before anything else.* Grabbing her phone, she hurried to the elevator which would take her to the lobby.

When Serena arrived at the gardens, she discovered Justice with the girls.

"Mom, look!" Jewel pointed to a rounded arch as high as the Torii gate's opening. On either side, Justice had secured Josef's six-foot-tall wooden nutcrackers. "Randi discovered a pair of these in the storage area."

"They are perfect," Serena replied.

"Ready?" Justice plugged in an electrical cord, and tiny white lights lit up the arch, giving off an inviting glow. "It works," he said, appearing satisfied with the job.

"The second arch is at the back entrance," Jewel said. "Come and see."

"Before we go anywhere, I need to speak with you and Jade." Serena motioned to her other daughter.

"Is something wrong?" Jade asked, leaving her dad's side to join them.

"Maybe." Serena stared at the girls. "You've given me two jobs." She held up the exact number of fingers to emphasize the point. "I'm supposed to sign books tomorrow on opening day. Is it possible to be the HR Director while working at a table?"

"We're on it," Jade answered, tilting her head toward the tearoom. "Jack offered to take your place. He's there now, setting up the table."

"Jack? He's busy with hotel security, girls."

"He volunteered, Mom," Jewel said. "He's the one who thought of it."

"That Jack." Justice shook his head. "One heck of a guy."

"Stop," Serena motioned with her hand, approaching Justice to prevent the girls from hearing. "I don't disparage you, so don't do it to Jack," she said under her breath.

"Kidding, Serena." Justice chuckled. "Can't you take a joke? Back in the day, you could."

Serena stayed silent. *That wasn't a joke. Justice wants approval from the girls, and I won't let him use Jack to get it.*

"Ms. Tate." Carmody bounced up next to her. "Reporting for duty."

"Hello, Carmody." Serena nodded. "I don't think you come to me for direction."

"Oh, but I do." Carmody grinned.

Carmody had a pleasant smile and friendly eyes. Serena believed she could adapt to having him around for brief periods of time. "Do tell," she said.

"Did you read the pamphlet?" Carmody raised his brows. "Well." He folded his arms. "I guess you didn't. I am to report any suspicious activity to you."

"What?" Serena took a deep breath.

"For instance." Carmody cocked his head toward the gingerbread people. "Them."

"What about *them*?"

"Since they're in costume, they could get away with a lot. I think you should get their names."

"Fine." Serena stared at the group. Some were not wearing their gingerbread heads. They appeared to be young adults from the college. "It seems like a perfect time to ask them. Go on, and report back to me."

"Yes, ma'am." Carmody saluted.

"And don't call me ma'am," Serena replied.

"Yeah, she hates that," Justice added.

Serena glared at him, and Justice shrugged. "Just trying to be helpful."

"I'm going to the tearoom," Serena said, and turned on her heel.

"Mom!" the girls called. "Where are you going?"

"If you need me, I'll be in the tearoom," Serena said over her shoulder.

Serena came to a halt at the entrance. Someone had set her author table right outside the restaurant and stacked her books at each end. They'd placed her poster behind the chair. A bowl overflowed with wrapped candy in red, silver and green foil. Her favorite pens sat in a row next to bookmarks, sporting her books' pictures and author name.

"Like it?" Jack asked, emerging from the tearoom.

"It's wonderful, Jack." Serena reached out to him, and he took her hand. "Thank you."

"You'll be close by in case I need you," Jack said.

Serena narrowed her eyes. "But you won't."

"Hopefully not." Jack held up a notebook. "But we need to be on the same page. Get it?" The corner of his mouth twitched.

"A writing joke." Serena smiled and nodded.

"When someone comes in with a complaint or to report something, we'll write the date and time, their name and complaint."

"Makes sense," Serena replied. "We'll have a reference if needed. May I?" She flipped over her hand to expose her palm, and Jack placed the book in it. Turning to the first page, Serena's eyes widened. "You already made three entries."

Serena read what Jack had written to herself, then said, "People are already complaining about Carmody, Josef and Sunita?"

"Don't worry, I handled it. Minor complaints." Jack lifted his shoulder.

Serena reread the entries. "Carmody is intrusive. Okay, he can work on that. Josef is yelling at people, and Sunita is bossy." She looked up at Jack. "Did you speak with them?"

"I did. Josef and I have a rapport after working together in the storage room. He's always loud. People will get used to him."

"And Sunita?"

"She's a confident, assertive woman who believes people should listen to her." Jack made a frustrated sound. "Sunita claimed certain spots for her dance troupe's performances and feels others should respect that."

"Wow. Okay. What about Carmody?"

"I left him for you." Jack chuckled.

"What? Why?" Serena placed a hand on her hip.

"He's Jewel's boyfriend."

"All the more reason for you to speak with him, Jack." Serena stared at him. "And he's not her boyfriend."

Jack pressed his lips together yet said nothing.

"Jack?" Serena tilted her head. "Are you hiding something from me?"

"It's nothing serious, Serena. They've gone on a few dates and mostly meet here." Jack stepped closer and lowered his voice. "I don't like that Felix kid. He has a knack for showing up wherever they are."

"You're scaring me, Jack." Serena inhaled and held her breath before letting it out. "I feel like I should put some names and pictures on my board."

"Your murder board?" Jack asked.

"That's what you call it?" Serena bit back a chuckle.

"Yes, and let's hope we don't need it." Jack nudged her. "Carmody is coming. Perfect time to speak to him."

"Ms. Tate, I have the gingerbread names."

"Cookie?" Serena asked. "Gingy, Gumdrop, Holly?"

"Very funny," Carmody said, but didn't laugh. "They're from the college. Drama department."

Serena thought it over before she spoke. "Don't you know most of them? You're in the drama department."

"Yes, I do."

"But you behaved as if they were strangers." Serena wondered why they didn't include Carmody in their gingerbread troupe and had to ask, "Why didn't you join their group?"

"I prefer to be a solo act," Carmody responded. "When they were in costume, I had no idea who they were. No one stands out."

"Makes sense. Thanks for the names," Serena said, tucking the paper into her notebook.

* * * *

Saturday morning the gardens hummed with activity. In less than ten minutes, the market would open to the public. Vendors and entertainers applied finishing touches to their areas, wanting the most magical experience for their guests.

Serena strolled alongside the girls, following the winding path to the ceremonial lighting of the Merry and Bright Christmas Market. A vibrant gathering of hotel staff and market participants assembled for the main event. Anticipation filled the air as they waited for the moment.

"Three. Two. One!" Jade and Jewel yelled and nodded at the electrician. He flipped the switch to illuminate the holiday lights.

The Pearl's gardens morphed into an enchanting holiday wonderland. The twinkling white lights made Serena feel like a kid again. Randi had informed Jade and Jewel that the hotel had purchased a snow machine for a winter wedding, and Nina granted permission for them to use it. Every hour, snow would fall for five minutes in the garden. A staff member was assigned to the task and dutifully activated the machine after the girls completed the countdown. Serena lifted her head and let the cold flakes land on her face.

Gingerbread people twirled to holiday music as they welcomed guests at the two entrances. Some escorted people through the lit arches to experience the market, while others waved at the passing crowd.

Carmody, now dressed as Selfie the Elf, acted as a cheerful tour guide. He handed out maps to the various shops and wished people happy holidays. The market buzzed with energy and excitement, filling Serena with pride and joy for her girls.

Between signing books, Serena found moments to join Jack at the Human Resource table, which remained quiet throughout the weekend. Jack made hourly rounds and returned with positive reports. No issues or complaints. Serena even consulted with Samurai, her fish, to gauge his feelings. He seemed content and relished the additional attention he received.

"We did it," Serena said to Jack. "It's Sunday night and the first weekend was a success." She leaned against him. "I'm exhausted."

Jack kissed the top of her head. "But it's a good kind of exhaustion."

They sat behind the table in the tearoom, taking in the silence.

"Hear that?" Serena asked.

"No. What did you hear?" Jack's voice held a touch of concern.

"Nothing." Serena giggled. "I guess we can close the books on this weekend and get ready for tomorrow."

"Not so fast," Sasha said, entering the tearoom. "I want to report someone."

"No-o-o." Serena rubbed between her eyes. "I thought we made it through two days unscathed."

"I want it on record that Josef Bauer is a bully and a pig," Sasha said in a defiant voice.

"Sit down." Serena pointed to the chair opposite her and Jack. "Tell us what happened."

"First, he asked me out for a drink after we closed on Saturday," Sasha huffed. "I shot him down, and he took offense. That big, hairy man won't leave me alone. Now, he has offered to carve a special nutcracker for me. Can you believe it?"

Serena puffed out her cheeks but couldn't hold back her laughter any longer. She looked at Jack, who was struggling to stay serious. "Come on, Jack. It's funny." Serena nudged him. "Josef and Sasha sitting in a tree," she sang.

"Stop, Serena." Sasha slapped her hands on the table. "It's not funny."

"I'd like to see the nutcracker once he delivers it," Jack said with a straight face.

Serena burst into a fit of laughter. "I would too. It might look like you, Sasha."

Sasha tapped the book. "Write it down, my dear cousin. Aren't you supposed to take every complaint seriously? We know nothing about him. The man could be a serial killer or a stalker."

Jack and Serena stopped laughing and gazed at each other. "Ooh," Serena said. "She's right."

"I'll start a background check on him right away," Jack replied. "If you'll excuse me." He rose from his seat and headed for the exit.

"I thought Jack was a security guard at the hotel," Sasha said. "He's capable of running background checks?"

"Between us?" Serena met her cousin's eyes. "Jack is much more than a security guard. He'll get the answers we need."

* * * *

The next morning, Sasha arrived at the tearoom with a nutcracker in hand. Serena gasped when Sasha handed it to her. The finely sculpted Black ballerina was beautiful. "Thank him and be done with it," Serena said.

"It's harassment," Sasha growled.

"It's lovely." Serena smiled.

"Write it down." Sasha pointed to the notebook. "I need to return to my shop."

"Did you discover the nutcracker there this morning?" Serena asked.

"Yes." Sasha swiped at a lock of hair which had fallen across her eye. "When you find me dead behind my shop, you'll know who did it."

"Who said anything about death or murder?" Serena widened her eyes. "It's a nutcracker."

"Serena." Sasha lowered her voice. "I heard about the recent killings in this hotel. Are you familiar with the saying, 'Things come in threes'? Well? Two murders and the year isn't over."

"Sasha," Serena hissed. "Don't start any rumors. The girls had a wonderful turnout this weekend, and every shop is doing well."

"Fine. I won't. I'm only saying it to you." Sasha glanced at her phone screen. "I need to go. We open in fifteen minutes."

Serena placed her head in her hands and let out a shuddering breath. She stared down at the table wondering how to solve her cousin's problem. *It appears Josef is attracted to Sasha. I can see why. She's attractive and creative. What am I to tell him?*

"Excuse me, Ms. Tate." Josef's voice broke into her thoughts.

"Josef!" Serena sat upright to find the man she called cinnamon bear in her mind, standing in front of her. "How can I help you?"

"It seems someone has stolen a box of my nutcrackers. I did inventory this morning and found one missing. It contained twenty nutcrackers. Perhaps a prank? If so, I would like them back."

Serena jotted the date, time and Josef's name with his complaint next to it. "I'll ask Jack to investigate this. Are you sure you didn't misplace the box?"

"Positive. I counted the stacked boxes last night. They were all there." Josef tapped the side of his head. "Plus, I keep each one I've made in here. I know who is missing. They are like my children."

I'm not writing that down. "I love the nutcracker you gave Sasha," Serena said, hoping to change the conversation and perhaps solve Sasha's problem.

"Oh, good. She received it. Does she like it?" Josef asked. "I named her little Sasha."

I'm not telling that to Sasha. "I think it's beautiful," Serena answered.

"But, does Sasha?"

"Well…yes…but Sasha would prefer if you didn't send any more gifts." Serena tried to be gentle. She didn't want to hurt his feelings but could see her words affected him.

Josef hung his head. "I understand. I will go now." He started to walk away, then stopped and returned to the table. "May I issue a complaint?"

"It's the reason I'm here," Serena replied, pasting on her best fake smile.

"The showman. Max Gruber. He is full of himself and looks down on me."

"I'm not a counselor, Mr. Bauer. Perhaps you can avoid him," Serena said.

"He says the same of me," Josef responded with a loud huff.

"That you need counseling?" Serena winced.

"No. That I am overbearing, loud and full of myself." Josef leaned in close to Serena. "He's threatened me. He wants to expose me."

A warning bell rang in Serena's head. *Please, no.* "How is he threatening you, Josef?"

"I have no time to explain." Josef checked the time. "The market opens soon."

Serena barely had time to blink before the man exited the tearoom. Josef brushed past Jack on his way out, ignoring Jack's greeting.

"What's with him?" Jack asked, jutting his thumb over his shoulder. He took the seat next to Serena and kissed her cheek. "Good morning."

"Hello, to you, too." Serena let out a breath. "Josef is feuding with Max Gruber. Did you have time to check Josef's background?"

"Yes, and I discovered something quite interesting. Josef may present himself as German, but he was born in Austria. He is half Austrian and half German. His family moved to Germany when he was twelve after he was dismissed from the Vienna Boys Choir."

Chapter Nine

"Whoa." Serena held up her hand. "Let's back up here. Sunita told me Max Gruber was in the Vienna Boys Choir. Do Josef and Max know each other?"

"Yes. It could be the reason Josef agreed to come to San Francisco," Jack replied.

"He knew Max was here and wants to confront him." Serena placed her head in her hands. "Everything was going so well. It was too good to be true."

"We need more information before we jump to conclusions," Jack said, rubbing Serena's back. "First, a brief history of the choir. Boys audition at nine or ten. If the selection committee chooses them, they enter the choir's grammar school. Besides the normal curriculum, they teach musical theory and other things pertaining to music. The choir divides the boys into four touring groups, named after Austrian composers."

"Don't tell me. Let me guess," Serena said, dropping her hands and folding them on the table. "Max and Josef are the same age, so they went to school together. The school assigned them to the same touring choir."

"Correct."

"They knew each other for three years." Serena tapped her chin. "Josef had two more years of eligibility but moved to Germany with his parents."

"Because of his dismissal, they had no reason to stay," Jack added.

"How did you discover the school dismissed him? That's huge." Serena tapped the table.

"I have my ways," Jack answered.

Serena realized he wouldn't share any information, so she asked, "What reason did they give for his expulsion?"

"The school sealed the records, and I can't find the reason they asked him to leave."

"He is awfully loud." Serena grimaced. "Perhaps he sang too loud and wouldn't blend in with the others."

"Only he can tell us," Jack replied with a smile.

"Or Max Gruber." Serena returned the smile.

"Hey." Jack pointed at her. "I see that look in your eye."

"Suddenly I'm in the mood to hear some holiday music. I should go to the choir's afternoon concert. Do you want to come with me?" Serena asked, glancing at Jack from the corner of her eye.

"Sure. I've got nothing better to do." Jack chuckled, then inhaled and slowly let out his breath. "Don't look now. Someone's coming to register a complaint."

Sunita stopped in front of the table and huffed. "Serena." She nodded. "Jack." She placed her hands on her hips. "I want to speak about the elf boy."

"You mean Selfie the Elf?" Serena corrected.

"If that is his name, then yes." Sunita stared at Serena. "That young man is a nuisance."

"Aren't all elves?" Serena hoped Sunita would laugh with her, but Sunita remained stoic. "Go on," she said.

"The elf insists he adds humor and lightness wherever he goes. But he's gone too far." Sunita narrowed her eyes. "He appears right before our performance and introduces the dance troupe."

"That seems harmless," Serena said.

"Wait." Sunita held up her pointer finger. "I am not finished. He does a terrible impersonation of our dance. He is mocking us."

"You think he's making fun of your culture?" Serena asked.

"Yes." Sunita bobbed her head with force.

"I'll speak with him," Jack said. "He won't interfere with your next performance."

"Thank you, Jack." Sunita motioned to her dancers, who stood motionless by the entrance. "It's done." She waved a hand, and they followed her out the door.

"Write it down, Jack." Serena slid the book in his direction. "I haven't had time to tell you about Josef's complaint. I'll talk. You write."

"I see his complaint here." Jack laid his hand under Serena's entry. "Max Gruber looks down on Josef. They have a beef." He shook his head and chuckled. "A beef? I haven't heard that expression in a while."

"I was in a hurry. Call it whatever you want. They don't like each other."

"Something happened at that school," Jack said. "When they met here, old resentments resurfaced."

"What if Max stole Josef's box of nutcrackers to mess with him?" Serena asked. "He might have hidden it in the storage area. Let's check."

"You can't," Jack said. "You must perform your duties as Human Resource Director." He winked. "But I can go."

"You're right. Text me if you find Josef's children."

Jack furrowed his brow. "Did I hear you correctly?"

"That is how Josef refers to them. His nutcrackers are his children. Just telling you like it is." Serena searched for a blank sheet of paper. "We can't be stuck here during market hours." She scribbled a message on the paper. "I'm going to close up shop whenever we need to leave."

"Okay." Jack nodded. "Make a sign for concert time." He started to leave, then changed his mind. "Forgot to ask. Did you get the names of those missing nutcrackers?"

Serena howled with laughter, loving that Jack had found his sense of humor again. "I wish I did," she replied. "I'll work on it." She motioned for him to leave. "Now go and find us some nutcrackers."

* * * *

Serena wriggled in her seat, wishing the concert would end. It had nothing to do with the music. She enjoyed the songs and hummed along with the choir. But as they sang the holiday tunes, she thought of more questions to ask Max Gruber. She strategized how to get him alone where they could speak openly.

"Serena?" Jack touched her arm. "The concert is over. Do you want to approach Max or shall I speak with him?"

"Let's go together," Serena answered. "Invite him to tea."

Once the crowd dispersed, Serena and Jack made their move. "Such a wonderful concert," Serena said.

"Thank you." Max bowed his head.

"I bet you'd love some quiet time away from the crowds." Serena gestured toward the tearoom. "Tea perhaps?"

"Well." Max glanced toward his students, then at Serena. "I suppose one cup wouldn't hurt. Then I must get back to rehearsing."

A taskmaster. Noted. Serena smiled. "We won't keep you long. Jack and I must get back to our command post, too."

Mia and Lily were leaving the tearoom as the trio arrived. "Hi, Serena," Lily said. "Jack." She nodded. "And Mr. Gruber. Mind if we borrow Serena for a minute?"

"No problem," Jack answered. "We'll get a table."

Lily pulled Serena away from the entrance. "Looks like we need a P.I.C. meeting. Mia and I stole a look at your book. Is your cousin okay?"

"She's fine." Serena waved her hand. "It's a misunderstanding. Josef likes her, and she wants no part of him. But, you're right. Let's meet and discuss the entries before things escalate."

"What about the missing box of nutcrackers?" Mia asked.

"Jack has looked for them but found nothing," Serena answered. She dropped her shoulders and let out a puff of air. "I'm letting my guard down, aren't I? So many red flags, and I'm ignoring them."

"Maybe not," Mia said. "But keep an eye on Carmody. Lily and I had tea with Sasha, and she said he's causing problems for some shopkeepers."

"Great." Serena used a deadpan voice. "Like what?"

"Minor infractions," Lily answered. "He's being mischievous, but the shopkeepers view him as a nuisance. He's taken gingerbread men from the cookie shop and dances with them. Since he's touched them, the woman who runs the shop doesn't want them back. He never pays for them, either."

"Hmm." Serena cocked her head. "I haven't had a complaint from the cookie shop."

"What about the pie and cake woman?" Mia asked. "I heard Selfie the Elf planted his face into one of her pies."

"And my daughter likes him?" Serena shook her head and touched her forehead.

"Maybe she never saw him do it?" Lily winced.

"Sorry. This isn't about Jewel and her relationship with Carmody. Thanks for telling me about these incidents. I'll speak with both women." Serena paused. "Or should I wait for them to report him?"

"Wait," Lily replied. "Let's meet Friday morning before the market opens for business. Mia and I will stroll the gardens during the week looking for anything suspicious. If Carmody steps out of line, we'll stop him."

"Wonderful. Friday morning we'll have a P.I.C. meeting. I may need something stronger than tea by then." Serena joked.

"You're doing a great job. Grandmother is thrilled about the market's success," Mia said. "And it's only been three days."

The women hugged and said their goodbyes, then Serena searched for Jack and Max. They weren't at Nina's special table, but the hostess had given them a quiet one on the back wall.

"Everything alright?" Jack asked when Serena reached the table.

"Girl talk," Serena said in an airy tone and took her seat.

"Max told me an interesting story," Jack said. "He knows Josef Bauer. They were in the Vienna Boys Choir together."

"Really?" Serena sat back, feigning surprise. "I thought Josef was German. He lived in Austria?"

"He is German. On his father's side," Max answered. "His father met Josef's mother on a business trip to Austria and relocated to the country. When Josef's father received a job offer in his native country, he moved the family to Germany."

"How old was Josef?" Serena asked.

"Twelve."

"I bet he hated to leave. Josef worked hard to become a choir member," Serena stated.

"It was time for him to go," Max answered, tilting his head to one side. "Sad, but true."

"Can you elaborate?" Jack asked.

"Och, it was long ago. I can barely remember." Max reached for his teacup.

"Were you friends?" Jack continued his questioning.

"Yes, and no." Max chuckled. "We all competed to be the best."

"I'm sorry, but I must ask," Serena said. "Do you look down on him? Josef has registered a complaint against you. I don't want an old rivalry to ruin this wonderful market."

Serena watched Max's body language as she spoke. He shifted in his seat, and his eyebrows rose high in his forehead for a split second. Max rubbed the side of his face and said, "Don't worry about me ruining the market. If something happens, blame Josef."

* * * *

Soon after closing time, a long line of market participants formed outside the restaurant. To get seated, tearoom patrons had to thread their way through the burgeoning crowd. Finally, a hostess asked the people in line to clear the entrance. Jack left the table and directed traffic, sending one person at a time to Serena.

Maggie Potts was first to come to the table. Her short, curly light brown hair entwined with strands of gray bounced around her head as she spoke. "That young man, the elf, has no manners. When I admonished him for stealing a pie, he declared it was part of his act. Do you believe it? He had no remorse at all."

"How much for the pie?" Serena asked, already familiar with the story.

"Twenty dollars." Maggie folded her arms. "Do you know what he did with the pie?" She didn't wait for Serena to respond. "He smashed his face into it and wasted an excellent dessert. I should charge him more than the standard price."

"I'll see you get the money." Serena let out a frustrated breath. "Next?"

By the time she got to Natasha, the gingerbread shopkeeper, Serena was exhausted.

"I don't want to get the elf in trouble," Natasha said. Her long, dark ponytail swung from side to side as she shook her head. "Could you ask him to be more mindful? He has talent, and for the most part, a fun and immersive act."

"I will speak with him," Serena said, noticing no one stood behind Natasha. *I'm done!*

"Thanks." Natasha left with a smile on her face and hadn't seemed offended by Carmody. She only wanted to report his antics.

Jack slipped in next to Serena and studied the notebook. "Most of the entries are about Carmody. Next is Josef. A few about Sunita and Max. All headstrong people. We'll need to keep them in check, Serena."

"I'll tell you who to keep in check," Sasha yelled upon reaching the table. "Josef Bauer." She slammed a nutcracker on the table

Serena jumped at the sound the wooden decoration made on the table. Dressed as a soldier, the nutcracker wore a forest green cape adorned with gold piping over a red jacket. Forest green pants and black laced boots completed the ensemble. A tall, black fur hat sat atop a mane of black hair. He sported a painted curled mustache, and his gaze was menacing.

"He's well made," Jack said, smiling up at Sasha.

"I'm not in the mood for jokes," Sasha announced, staring at Jack. "This needs to stop. Now."

"Sasha," Serena said in a stage whisper. "I spoke to Josef. He promised to leave you alone."

"Well, look how that turned out." Sasha gestured to the nutcracker. "At least the ballerina was pretty. This thing looks like…"

"There he is!" Josef's voice boomed throughout the restaurant. "Oh, my poor Henrik, where have you been? I am grateful to you, Sasha. Thank you for finding him."

"I did not *find* him, Josef," Sasha replied. "When I returned from the storage room, he was sitting next to my painting of the Eiffel Tower at Christmas." She pointed at Josef. "Leave me alone."

"I did not put him there. You must believe me," Josef pleaded.

"Is Henrik…" Jack paused, and Serena grasped his arm to keep him from laughing. "One of the missing nutcrackers?"

"Yes. Exactly." Josef nodded.

"One down. Nineteen to go," Serena whispered. She met Josef's eyes and said, "Look, Josef, we'll take your word this time, but if anyone else receives an unexpected nutcracker, we'll need to investigate. For now, you're free to go."

Josef swept up the nutcracker and walked out of the tearoom.

"What are you? A cop?" Jack whispered.

"I learned from the best," Serena said, then looked at her cousin. "I'm sure he meant no harm."

"We'll see." Sasha narrowed her eyes. "But you better watch out for him."

Chapter Ten

Tuesday morning, Serena woke up earlier than Jade and Jewel. They had celebrated their success with the choir and gingerbread people late into the evening, so Serena wasn't surprised. She hoped the group had gotten to know the real Carmody, beyond his role as Selfie the Elf, and developed a genuine rapport. *With any luck, today will go smoothly.* Serena stepped into the shower and finished before the twins' alarm sounded.

Serena had updated the girls on the complaints, and Jewel offered to handle Carmody's case. She promised he would pay Maggie Potts for the ruined pie. Jewel had giggled when Serena read the entry to her, and Serena worried that her daughter didn't see the gravity of the situation. *Young love.* She sighed as she dried off and did her hair and makeup.

"Mom?" Jade pounded on the door. "Are you finished?"

Serena swung back the door. "Yes. It's all yours. I'm meeting Jack for breakfast, so I'll leave in a few minutes."

"Tearoom?" Jade asked.

"Actually, we are going to the dining room," Serena said, touching her hair.

"Ooh, fancy," Jade touched the back of her hair.

"Mom?" Jewel called from the bedroom.

"Yes?"

"Carmody will pay Maggie at the end of the market today. He doesn't want to interfere with her customers and sales during market hours."

He should have considered that before planting his face in a pie. "Okay," Serena answered. "Thanks for telling me."

Hurrying to the elevator, Serena hoped for a quiet breakfast with Jack prior to the market's opening. Once inside the cubicle, she glanced down at the white silk blouse and black pants she wore, hoping she looked suitably dressed for the more upscale restaurant. She'd chosen the look for its style and comfort since she'd wear it for the rest of the day. Hopefully, the camel and black-toed low-heeled shoes gave the outfit a classic look. Serena felt satisfied with her choices as she stepped from the elevator into the lobby.

When she entered the dining room, a hostess immediately greeted her. "Hello, Ms. Tate. Mr. Ando is already seated," the woman said. "Please follow me."

As Serena bypassed the tables, she thought she heard a familiar voice. *Justice?* She looked to her right and held her breath. Justice sat at a cozy table for two, leaning toward her cousin Sasha with a teasing grin. "Sasha!" Serena said in a shocked tone.

"Serena." Sasha put her coffee cup into its saucer. "What are you doing here?" She appeared surprised and, if Serena read her correctly, guilty.

"I am meeting Jack for breakfast," Serena answered as she made her way to their table. "I should ask the same of you."

"We didn't plan this," Justice said, motioning toward Sasha, then himself. "It just happened."

"Totally impromptu." Sasha agreed. "I would have told you, Serena, really."

Serena held up her hand like a stop signal. "Don't." She glared at Justice. "Of all the women in the world?" She shook her head and turned away to search for Jack.

Serena didn't need to look far. Jack was already coming to her rescue. "Hey, I see you made a detour. Hello, Sasha. Justice," he said politely. "Come on, Serena. I've ordered you a pot of tea."

Jack guided Serena to their table. "Sorry, I never saw them. I would have warned you," he said in a kind voice. "Are you upset?"

"Yes," Serena answered. "But not jealous. It came as a shock, nothing more." *Sasha assured me she wasn't interested in Justice, yet she flirted with him. Now they're having breakfast.* "We're all adults. If they choose to see each other, I can't stop them." Tears welled in her eyes. "I guess I don't know my cousin as well as I thought."

"Sorry." Jack pulled out her chair. "At least you can't see them from here."

"Jack, you are being too considerate." Serena gazed at him across the table.

"I put myself in your place, Serena. What if I saw my ex-wife with a good friend or my brother? I'd feel the same."

"Thanks for understanding." Serena pointed to the teapot. "Oolong?"

* * * *

"I am happy to report that Carmody paid Maggie twenty dollars for the pie," Jewel said at the end of the market day. "She thanked him, and they parted as friends."

"Friends?" Serena closed one eye as she looked up at her daughter, who stood on the other side of the Human Resource table.

"Okay." Jewel exhaled loudly. "They were polite to each other, and Carmody promised to stay away from her stand until closing day." Jewel rolled her eyes. "Old people."

"Jewel." Serena frowned. "The woman is probably in her fifties."

"Like I said, old people. The older generation can't take a joke."

Surprised by Jewel's new attitude, Serena said, "What?"

"Come on, Mom. You've heard what they say about the older generation. They destroyed the economy yet benefitted from it at the same time. They don't understand why younger people like me can't find a job, buy a home or even afford to move out of their parents' house."

"You're making a generalization, Jewel."

"All the kids feel that way, Mom."

"Kids? As in Carmody?"

"No. All of them. The choir. The gingerbread people."

""I thought you went out for fun, not to criticize older people," Serena said, shaking her head.

"Felix brought it up, and it led to a great discussion."

"That's what college is for, I guess," Serena replied. "Now, can we get back to Maggie?"

"Sure."

"Can I cross her complaint off my list?"

"Not so fast." Maggie entered the tearoom, waving a nutcracker over her head with gusto. She shook it so hard the wooden mouth opened and closed repeatedly.

Serena swore she spotted something stuck to the bottom of its stand. *Apples?* "Oh, no." She rubbed her forehead. "Please tell me Maggie is not holding a nutcracker."

"You see a nutcracker," Jewel said. "I've got to go."

"Not so fast, young lady," Serena said in a stern tone. "Stay here. This may concern someone you know." She looked at Maggie. "May I help you?"

"I turned away to pack up the leftovers," Maggie yelled. "And when I returned for the final pie, it had this stuck inside."

"Are those apples?" Serena winced as she pointed to the nutcracker's stand.

"Yes." Maggie dropped her shoulders. "I promised Josef I'd save some cherry strudel for him. I completely forgot and sold out. When he came to retrieve his package,

I apologized and returned his money. But no." Her curls shook as she shouted. "That was not good enough. Josef had to show his anger." She shoved the nutcracker in Serena's face. "I see this as a threat."

The scent of cinnamon and apples invaded Serena's senses, which made her stomach growl and reminded her she hadn't eaten since breakfast. She blinked and forced herself to focus. The soldier nutcracker had the same scowling face as the one Sasha received. The only difference was the color of his uniform.

"You're saying Josef threatened you because he didn't get his cherry strudel?" Serena inquired.

"Absolutely." Maggie let out a puff of air. "First an elf harasses me, now this man. What are you going to do about it?"

"Are you sure it was Josef?" Sunita asked, walking up to Maggie.

Where did she come from? Serena checked for a line and didn't see one.

"Anyone could have done it." Sunita narrowed her eyes. "I heard someone stole a box of Josef's nutcrackers."

"You think the elf did it?" Maggie asked in a frustrated voice. "Not Josef?"

"Let the elf, I mean Carmody, defend himself," Jewel said. "I'll go get him."

"And while you're at it, find Josef," Serena said. "I want them both here." She grabbed her phone and texted Jack to get to the tearoom pronto. "How can I help you, Sunita?" Serena asked, staring at the woman.

"Maggie flew by me with the nutcracker in hand, mumbling words I cannot repeat. I came to support her," Sunita answered.

Serena placed her elbows on the table and leaned forward. "Did you see the crime happen?" *I called it a crime. What am I thinking?*

"No." Sunita shook her head.

"Any witnesses?" Serena looked at Sunita and waited. "No?" She turned to the other woman. "Maggie, what about you? Witnesses?"

"None," Maggie answered.

"There is my Greggor," Josef exclaimed, pushing Jack and Carmody aside as the three entered the tearoom. "Oh, my sweet boy, what have they done to you?" He examined the nutcracker, checking for damage.

"*You* did it." Maggie poked Josef's arm. "You big oaf. You sent that thing as a message."

Oblivious to Maggie's words or the jab of her finger, Josef gestured to the bottom of the nutcracker. "What is this?"

"Apples." Serena bit her lip. "Josef, did you do this?"

"Do what?"

"Stick this nutcracker into one of Maggie's apple pies."

"No. Greggor is one of the missing nutcrackers," Josef responded. "Why would I do that to one of my children?"

"He's lying," Sunita said. "No one counted how many boxes he brought to the show. We only have his word he lost one."

"Sunita," Serena said. "Thank you for your help. If you wouldn't mind, I'd like to speak with Josef, Carmody and Maggie."

"This way," Jack said, taking Sunita's elbow and guiding her to the tearoom exit. "You've been quite helpful."

Serena pointed to the three chairs across from her. "Sit."

After fifteen minutes of cross-examination, Serena gave up, realizing she'd made no progress. She dismissed the group, promising them that she and Jack would interview other market participants.

"I need a nap," Serena told Jack once they were alone.

"I'm with you." Jack chuckled.

"Mom?" Jewel slid out from the shadows. "I need to share something with you."

Serena motioned to a chair. "Please have a seat."

"I'd rather stand." Jewel wrapped her arms around herself.

"You can tell us anything, Jewel," Jack said.

"Hey, that's my line." Serena nudged Jack. She smiled at Jewel for encouragement. Her daughter's serious expression made her heart pound. "Go ahead."

"Last night…when we were out…." Jewel looked over her shoulder and turned back. "Carmody was telling us about an old movie he had recently seen. A kid in high school used an apple pie for something." She raised her eyebrows.

"We get it," Serena said. "Say no more."

"That's where he got the idea of putting his face in a pie. Not like the movie, obviously." Jewel shifted from one foot to the other. "I don't want to accuse him, but what if Carmody stuck the nutcracker in the apple pie as one more trick to play on Maggie? Perhaps it was a parting gift. His actions weren't driven by malice, more like a mischievous elf prank."

"We'll take it into consideration," Serena said. "But if what you're saying is true, Carmody is also guilty of stealing Josef's nutcrackers. Think long and hard about what you said. Is Carmody who you think he is?"

"Mom." Jewel took a step toward the table. "I am a good judge of character. I understand what you are saying. No way did Carmody steal a box of nutcrackers, so he's not guilty of putting one in the pie."

"Let's table this discussion," Serena replied, knowing Jewel would keep defending Carmody. "If I can be a mom for a moment, instead of Human Resource Director, may I suggest you find your sister, have dinner and go to bed. Tell Carmody you'll see him tomorrow."

"Okay." Jewel headed for the door without saying another word.

"That was easy," Serena said and faced Jack. "Does Jewel assume Carmody is guilty?"

"I can't say for certain, but you gave her something to reflect on." Jack took Serena's hand. "Let's save it for tomorrow. What if we leave the hotel and go Christmas shopping?"

"That sounds like heaven," Serena answered. "But let's eat first."

* * * *

"Should we start with the nutcrackers?" Jack suggested in a playful tone. "Interview them one at a time." He pointed to the salt on the table and stooped to its level. "When did you last speak with Greggor?"

Serena reached for the pepper and placed it in front of her. "Was Henrik really missing with nineteen other nutcrackers or is he part of Josef's nefarious plan?" She giggled. "I laugh, but it's not funny. Should we be more serious about this, Jack? It's the holiday season, and I want to enjoy it and not worry about nutcrackers who threaten people."

"Giving up your detective badge?" Jack winked.

"I wasn't aware I had one." Serena fluttered her lashes. "Are you making me an honorary member?"

"Of course," Jack answered. "And to your point, I am still looking into this nutcracker situation. It seems harmless, but someone is sending a message. Now that we confronted the alleged suspects, it should stop."

"What if it doesn't?" Serena grimaced.

"You already know the answer, Serena." Jack covered her hand with his. "We should stay ahead of this."

"It still might be a prank," Serena said. "Carmody can take things too far. He may see it as hilarious and won't stop. If Josef is using nutcrackers to threaten people, it changes things. It's not so funny anymore."

As she finished her last bit of dinner, Serena had a thought. *Why didn't this occur to me earlier? Josef's shop is by the pond. I need to visit Samurai.*

"I recognize that look," Jack said before Serena could speak. "We can shop another day. Shall we stroll through the market tomorrow morning before opening the HR table? You can start your Christmas shopping there."

"It sounds wonderful," Serena answered and closed one eye. "Did you read my mind?"

"I might possess the power." Jack smiled. "But your facial expression gave you away."

"I shouldn't be that easy to read." Serena hung her head and glanced at Jack from the corner of her eye. "I won't be long. Can we meet in your room later?"

"You can stay the night if you wish. Isn't it getting a little crowded in your suite? Nina would have given the girls their own room. All you needed to do was ask."

"No." Serena shook her head. "Nina's done enough. Besides, I want the girls where I can see them, especially at night."

"I hear you. I'll pay the bill if you want to go," Jack said.

"Thanks, I'll get the next one." Serena rounded the table and kissed Jack on the cheek. "There's more of that to come."

Serena hurried through the restaurant and out to the main lobby. People strolled in and out of the gardens, enjoying the festive decor despite the closed shops. The holiday spirit filled the air along with the Christmas music piped through the hotel. Serena headed for the garden's front entrance and patted one of the giant nutcrackers as she passed through the Torii gate. The soothing sound of the pond's fountain greeted her ears, and upon arrival, she saw no one. *I've got the place to myself. No one will see me talking to a fish.*

"Samurai," Serena whispered.

The red and white koi sprang from the water, appearing happy to see her.

"Hello, to you, too." Serena leaned on the railing. "I wish you could answer more than yes and no questions but here goes. Do you know who Josef is? The Nutcracker King?"

Samurai swam in circles and popped up his head.

"Great. Did he lose a box of nutcrackers?"

Serena had never witnessed a delayed response from Samurai, which caused her to worry more. The koi lifted his head and his tail. "Does that mean you're not sure?" she asked.

The fish raised his head above the water.

"Since his shop is here, you've heard him talk about the missing box, right?" *Yes, again.* "Yet, there's no concrete proof." *He agrees.* "Okay, I'll stop asking questions and let you get some rest. Next time, we'll see who you know from the market, like Carmody."

Samurai swam in a giant circle and sprang high into the air.

"Oh? You've met him and appear to like him," Serena whispered. "Interesting." She patted the railing. "I'll see you tomorrow, Sam. Right now, it's Serena and Jack time."

Chapter Eleven

"What was that?" Jack jerked into a sitting position.

"It's my alarm. Sorry. I should have told you I set it," Serena answered. "I wanted to get up early."

"What time is it?"

"Six."

"What's the plan?" Jack covered his eyes with his arm when Serena turned on the bedside lamp.

"I want to check out Josef's stand before he gets there." Serena faced Jack. "Time to put on our detectives' capes." She bounced to the edge of the bed. "I can be ready in fifteen minutes. Let's leave at six-thirty."

Jack rolled to his side and groaned. "Can't talk you out of this, can I?"

"Nope."

"Did you ever hear of breaking and entering?"

"We're not doing that. We'll just look around." Serena crawled across the mattress to where Jack lay and kissed his shoulder. "Come on. We're wasting time."

When Serena emerged from the bathroom, ready for action, Jack was nowhere in sight. She searched under the bed and in the closet. "Nope."

"Looking for me?"

Serena gulped and turned toward Jack. "You scared me! Where did you go?"

"Down to the security office. Our facility includes a locker room and showers." Jack pointed to her black long-sleeved t-shirt tucked into her black skinny jeans. "Dressing the part?" he joked.

"Yes, and since that black t-shirt and jeans is your usual attire, I guess we're ready." Serena chuckled, grabbing her purse. She dug inside and pulled out a gaudy holiday necklace. "I'll wear this later. Jazz up the outfit."

Jack peeked into her bag. "I hope there isn't one for me."

"What if there was?" Serena closed one eye. "Would you wear it for me?"

"Only in certain situations." Jack winked. "Come on. It's six-thirty. I've checked the cameras, and no one is in the gardens. By seven, the shopkeepers will start restocking their shelves for the day."

Serena slipped her hand into Jack's. "I love you for going along with my crazy schemes."

"And I just love you."

* * * *

"We must rule out Josef or make him our prime suspect," Jack said. "Someone is framing him or he's the culprit."

"You read my thoughts again, Jack Ando," Serena replied, walking around the outside of the nutcracker shop.

Before arriving, Josef had sent his design and specifications to the girls. Justice had done a magnificent job bringing his vision to life. He had painted the shop a rich brick red both inside and out and designed two realistic display windows on the exterior walls. On each shelf, he'd painted winter scenes of snow and pine trees with nutcrackers scattered throughout. Above the front entrance, Josef had requested a "Merry Christmas" sign written in German.

"Josef doesn't leave much behind when the workday ends," Jack said.

"Except for two locked boxes, Jack." Serena pointed to the back wall. "We need to see what's inside."

"What do you think you're doing?" a voice asked from outside the shop.

"Nina!" Serena placed her hand over her heart. "Oh, my, you scared me."

"Well?" Nina stared at her.

"We're doing a safety check," Serena answered.

"Bull."

Did Nina just say bull? "I haven't seen you in days, Nina," Serena said, hoping to distract her. "Where have you been?"

"Busy with hotel business, but I'm here now."

"Have you heard about the missing nutcrackers?"

"Yes. Someone is using them to threaten people."

"So. You believe there's a threat." Serena made eye contact with Jack.

"I do." Nina stepped inside the shop. "Now, what can I do to help?"

"Jack was about to break into those locked boxes," Serena answered. "I'm sure he's done it many times before."

"Serena." Jack looked at her, then faced Nina. "With your permission, of course."

"Do what you must," Nina answered. "I'll watch for any early visitors or shopkeepers."

Serena held back a giggle. After she recovered from the shock of being caught, she noticed Nina's outfit. *Black blouse and dress pants. She planned to help us, but how did she know we were here?*

Nina paced in front of the shop, and Serena joined her. "I hope Josef is innocent. He thinks of his nutcrackers as his children."

"Who do his dirty work." Nina paused and glanced into the shop.

"You think he's guilty?"

"Until he's proven innocent." Nina stared at her. "Have you learned nothing, Serena? Your emotions are clouding your judgment again."

"You're right, Nina. Why do I keep doing that?"

"Because you are kindhearted, my dear." Nina patted Serena's arm. "Not to say I'm not." She chuckled, and Serena joined in.

"I've got the small box open," Jack announced. "It's mostly paperwork, but I found an inventory sheet."

"Great news," Serena replied. "Does it tell how many boxes he shipped to The Pearl?"

"Twenty." Jack looked up at Serena. "Next stop is the storage room."

"Josef could have hidden the box," Nina said. "This proves nothing."

Serena dropped her shoulders. "She's right, Jack. Plus, he's sold some of his inventory, and the hotel recycles those boxes. Anything else in there?"

"An old picture," Jack answered. "Of the Vienna Boys Choir. Serena, come and see if you agree with me. Josef circled someone's face and drew an X through it. I believe it's Max Gruber."

Nina beat Serena to Jack's side. "It's him," she acknowledged.

"Serena?" Jack held up the photo.

Serena squinted and took a closer look. "I agree, and it proves he has a grudge against Max." She looked at her two co-conspirators. "Yet he's done nothing to him."

"There's still time," Nina stated. "The market stays open for another week and a half." She turned to Jack. "Be vigilant, please. I want this Christmas market to succeed. It's popular and profitable."

"Yes." Jack bowed his head. "I'll do hourly strolls and alert the security staff."

* * * *

Serena assured Jack she would man the Human Resource table if he wanted to visit the security office.

Within minutes of taking her seat, a person arrived with a nutcracker in hand.

"I came to support Maggie Potts yesterday, and I get this as a warning today," Sunita said. She set the nutcracker, designed like Mrs. Claus, on the table.

"I'd keep her. She's cute," Serena said and bit her lip after seeing Sunita's expression. She reached for the notebook. "You believe Josef sent you a message by placing Mrs. Claus…"

"In our first dance spot," Sunita answered. "I brought two witnesses to collaborate. Girls?"

Anna and Sophie Wagner shuffled forward.

"You are part of the choir," Serena said. "Sisters, if I recall."

Anna, the older one, answered with a "yes".

"Did you see anyone put the nutcracker in the dance area?" Serena questioned the girls.

"No, it was already there," Sophie said. "Anna and I stopped to look at it, and Sunita arrived after us."

"See," Sunita said. "They came upon it before I did."

"You think Josef left it?" Serena tried to act concerned.

"Or the other fellow. The elf. Jack brought those two scoundrels to the tearoom while I was testifying on Maggie's behalf. They saw me. They heard me. One of them sent me a warning. They want to shut me up."

"Okay," Serena said. "I've got all I need. Sunita, please leave Mrs. Claus here as evidence. Girls, would you mind staying a few minutes?" She stared at Sunita, who appeared hesitant to leave.

"Sure," Anna replied.

After Sunita exited the tearoom, Serena asked the girls, "How's everything? Are you enjoying the experience?"

"Um." Anna bit her lip. "I thought you were going to ask questions like the police do."

"I'm not the police. Just an interested mom."

The girls seemed to relax, and Sophie said, "I love your daughters, Ms. Tate. For freshmen, they have it all together. I'm still finding my way."

"You will find your way," Serena assured her. "I'd like to hear your opinion about the nutcracker incidents."

"Leo said it's funny," Sophie replied with a smile.

"Leo?" Serena pointed at her. "He's in the choir."

"Yes, a sophomore," Sophie said dreamily.

"He's a stupid boy." Anna nudged her. "Leo needs to grow up."

Interesting. I need to examine the choir more closely. Boys that age seek attention by doing silly things. "Anyone else need to grow up? Like Carmody?" Serena couldn't resist asking.

"Carm is okay," Anna answered. "Alex, Felix and Leo." She rolled her eyes.

"Say no more." Serena chuckled. "I won't keep you, girls. Thanks for helping. Are you sure you didn't see anyone leave the designated dance area when you arrived?" Both solemnly shook their heads. "Fine. You're free to go."

* * * *

Serena didn't expect a lot of complaints during market hours. *Too many witnesses could observe the nutcracker bandit in action. He strikes in the early morning or after hours. Ooh, I need to tell Jack I named him. Where is he? It's past lunch hour.* She reached for her phone and texted him. *Where are you?*

"Right here." Jack wiggled his phone in the air. "Did you need me?"

"Not exactly." Serena patted the chair next to her. "Sit." After Jack slid onto the seat, Serena said, "I named the suspect. Wait for it." Excited, she shook her fists in the air. "The Nutcracker Bandit."

"It's good but keep it as a title for your next book," Jack teased.

"Maybe I will. I'm still working on *Secrets, Suspicions, and Stolen Pearls.* That title came to me while Linda held me hostage last summer. She stabbed Amber in the back and thought she got away with it until she realized we knew. Taking me hostage was smart. She could manipulate Nina into doing her bidding or so she thought."

"You could think about books at a time like that?" Jack sat back and wrinkled his brow. "Kudos to you."

"It provided me with the inspiration I needed," Serena said with a grin. "But I prefer to be motivated to write in a safer setting."

"Very true." Jack squeezed her hand. "You've been skipping lunch, so I ordered those little sandwiches you like."

"Cucumber?"

"Yes, and a pot of tea."

"What about you?"

"I already ate. After I left the security office, I stopped in the restaurant for an impossible burger. Needed some fuel before I searched the storage room."

"Find anything?"

"No, but it made me think. Why would the bandit leave the box in the storage room? Someone would eventually discover it."

"Ooh, Jack, you said bandit." Serena wrapped her hands around his tattooed arm.

"Did I? How about if we close for an hour and stroll the market after lunch?" Jack arched his brow.

"I'd love it," Serena answered. "I want to find something for Mama. She's been here twice and raved about the merchandise."

"Would she like a handmade German nutcracker?" Jack asked, raising his brows. He gestured to Mrs. Claus, who stared at them with her beady eyes.

"She would." Serena brought the nutcracker closer to them and examined its features. "I haven't told her about the nutcracker case."

"So now it's a case?"

"It is until we solve it."

Eve, a new server at the restaurant, arrived with Serena's lunch. When she finished the tea and sandwiches, Serena rose from her chair. "Time to visit Josef's shop."

Josef and Max appeared to be in a heated discussion as Jack and Serena approached the shop. Serena slid her eyes towards Jack to see if he agreed, and he bobbed his head. She searched for nearby guests, hoping to preserve the atmosphere of the Merry and Bright Christmas Market, but found no one.

"Gentlemen," Jack said, stepping in between them. "Can I help?"

"Just reminiscing, Jack," Max said in a normal tone.

"More like twisting the truth." Josef appeared combative.

Serena heard someone snicker and looked beyond the men. Max's choir stood waiting for him by the pond. Approaching them, she said, "Nothing more to see here. I suggest you head to the stage and get ready for your performance. Mr. Gruber should only be a few more minutes."

Returning to the shop, Serena overheard Jack say, "This isn't the right time or place to air old grudges. I suggest you avoid each other until the market ends. After that, feel free to continue your vendetta."

"I did nothing. He." Max pointed to Josef. "Interrupted me on the way to the stage. I did not come here to fight, and I promise to stay away from him." He strode away like a man on a mission.

"Josef," Serena said. "Why did you stop Max? He and the choir have a performance."

"I want him to clear my name. The school unjustly expelled me from the choir. Only he knows the true story."

"Why after all these years?"

"My expulsion tarnished my reputation for many years. I made a promise to clear my name before I died." Josef wiped a tear escaping his eye.

"I'm sorry," Serena said. "But may I remind you, this is a market and not a place for your personal vendetta. You are selling your wonderful German nutcrackers. I came to buy one for my mother."

Josef perked up at the sound of a sale. "Oh, I have the perfect one for you." He gestured to a row of Mrs. Clauses painted in various skin tones.

"I love the subtle differences. Not one looks like the one Sunita brought to my office," Serena replied, keeping her eyes on the nutcrackers.

"Sunita never bought one," Josef said.

"No, she didn't." Serena met his eyes. "She found one this morning in her dance area."

"Oh, no. Was it my Cassandra?" Josef asked.

Serena wrinkled her brow. "No, it was Mrs. Claus."

"Cassandra is the only missing Mrs. Claus. It must be her. Did someone use her to threaten Sunita?" Josef asked.

"Was it you?" Jack gave Josef a questioning look.

"No, absolutely not."

We won't get a confession, so I better change the subject. "I'll take this one," Serena said, choosing the nutcracker which most reminded her of her mother. "I'm done shopping, Jack. Let's return to the tearoom."

"I will come to retrieve Cassandra after hours," Josef stated.

"No. You won't." Serena looked at Jack. "We should keep it as evidence."

"I agree." Jack nodded as he made eye contact with Josef. "Sorry, but this nutcracker is part of a criminal investigation."

Chapter Twelve

"A criminal investigation?" Serena asked, as she and Jack walked to the tearoom.

"It sounded good, right?" Jack ushered Serena to their table. "I wanted to instill some fear into him." He took Mrs. Claus in hand and studied the nutcracker. "I'm going to take this to the security office, label it and lock it up. Moving forward, we must handle these with greater care."

"You want to check the nutcracker for fingerprints?" Serena grimaced.

"Yes. I don't want to involve the police, but I may need their services."

"True." Serena let out a breath. "Then we have to deal with Bill Mitchell."

"Exactly." Jack gave her a salute as he left the tearoom.

At one time, Jack and Detective Bill Mitchell worked together at the SFPD. Bill never liked Jack and made an unauthorized deal with him. If Jack resigned, Bill would release a suspect Serena and Jack needed for leverage against the true supermodel killer. It had succeeded, and they got the confession, but Jack had to sacrifice one of his passions, detective work, to achieve it.

Despite Bill's hopes, solving a high-profile murder case never led to a promotion. Serena sensed he blamed her for interfering and costing him the advancement he believed he deserved. Now, whenever he discovered any issues at The Pearl, no matter how minor, he'd come to the hotel and start asking questions. If he heard about the request to check fingerprints on a nutcracker, he would arrive within the hour.

Serena checked her watch, surprised by how late it had gotten. On weekdays, the market closed earlier. Seven p.m. instead of nine. *I'll text the girls and see if they want to meet for dinner. Probably not. The gingerbread people have become part of their group. I wonder if Jade has a crush on one of them. Andre, I bet.*

A pile of plastic bags appeared before Serena. She blinked and saw Jack standing on the other side of the table. "You're back?'

Jack placed his hand on the bags. "If we get any more evidence, it goes in these bags." He held up labels. "Write date and name of who brought them on here."

"And stick it on the bag?" Serena grinned. "Got it."

After Jack took his seat, he asked, "What were you thinking about when I came in? You seemed miles away."

"Dinner."

Jack chuckled. "Me, too."

"I texted the girls but haven't heard from them yet."

"Jade, Andre, Jewel and Carmody are going out."

"A double date?" Serena widened her eyes. "Why am I always the last to find out?"

"No one tells their mom anything at that age. I didn't."

"You were in the service, Jack. Hard to do from a distance. The girls are right outside this door." Serena cocked her head toward the entrance. "I hope they have fun," she said with a sigh.

"They will. Try not to worry about them," Jack replied and covered her hand with his. "While at the security office, I assigned a few people to study the garden footage from the start of the market until now. I've gone through some, but I want it all checked. We don't have cameras everywhere, but I hope to find the culprit through the footage."

"You mean bandit." Serena folded her arms.

"Okay, fine, bandit." Jack rolled his eyes. "I have one more idea, Serena. I'm going to follow Josef. I'll leave here before the market closes and find a spot where I can watch him without being seen."

"Ooh, a stakeout," Serena said, rubbing her hands together.

"I said *I* would do this."

"Sure." Serena nodded. "Until I shut down the office and join you."

Jack made a noise in his throat as if to protest, but a loud voice caused him to turn away from Serena.

"Enough of this nonsense!" Max bellowed after entering the tearoom. He slammed a nutcracker on the table. "This is a nutcracker king. Proof that Josef is behind it all. Think." He tapped the side of his head. "Josef Bauer. The Nutcracker King."

The king stood proudly in front of Serena. He wore a golden crown on his head, and Serena imagined Josef lovingly placing it atop the nutcracker's white hair. His indigo coat with gold shoulder braiding hung over raspberry knickers with gold trim. Black boots completed the outfit. Serena wanted to reach out and twirl his white mustache, even though she knew Josef had painted it onto his face.

Jack whipped open a plastic bag and covered the decoration before anyone could touch it. "Is there a witness?" he asked.

"No." Max shook his head.

"Did you argue with anyone besides Josef today?" Jack questioned.

"Just Carmody but it wasn't a confrontation. I asked him to stop dancing around my singers. It's distracting."

"Anyone else?" Jack gazed up at him after completing his task.

"My choir?" Max appeared frustrated. "They get too silly when Carmody appears. I stressed the importance of being professional singers." He glanced away. "I needed to lecture them…in a stern voice."

"So," Serena said. "Josef, Carmody and all of your choir are suspects."

"No…well…maybe…stop!" Max ran his hand through his graying blonde hair.

"Max, take a seat," Jack said. "Tea is on its way."

Serena glanced at Jack, wondering what he had planned. He gave her a "trust me" look. A server carried a tray with a pot of tea and three teacups and stopped at their table. She set the cups down and poured the tea. "Anything else?" she asked, serving each person a cup.

"Thanks, Eve, we're good," Jack said, and waited for her to leave. "Max, you need to tell us more of the history between you and Josef. I feel you left something out."

"There is nothing to tell." Max stared into his teacup.

"According to Josef, he has additional information," Serena said. "It seems you're the only witness to an event that occurred during your school years. Whatever happened got Josef expelled from the university."

"It is so long ago. Why does it matter?" Max lifted a hand.

"It does to Josef." Serena narrowed her eyes.

"Fine. I will tell you, but we cannot do anything to fix it." Max stirred his tea. "I benefitted from being in the choir, and Josef did not. It is as simple as that."

"That is hard to believe." Serena gazed at him until Max fidgeted in his seat and rolled his shoulders. "How did you benefit?" she asked.

"For one thing, the university offered me this job. I oversee the music department of this prestigious place. Josef only carves nutcrackers for a living."

"I'm sure he has other options." Serena made a tsking sound.

"Josef loved music. His dream was to pursue it as a career, or at least work part time in the field."

"Why can't he?" Serena insisted.

Max dropped his head. "Fine. I will tell you what happened." He studied the tea in his cup for what seemed like hours, then finally said, "Our choir director had chosen a boy, Hans, and Josef to vie for a solo. If unable to compete, due to grades or illness, I would serve as the alternate."

Serena looked at Jack from the corner of her eye. She wondered if he, too, realized Max was finally telling the true story. She didn't want to interrupt or stop Max's train of thought. Jack nudged her, acknowledging what she had assumed, and she returned the tap.

Max cleared his throat. "Hans wanted Josef to withdraw from the competition. He believed he could defeat me, but not Josef. I stumbled upon them in a stairwell locked in a heated argument. Hans initiated a physical fight, catching Josef off-guard with the first punch. He landed several hits before Josef responded with a single blow to Hans' face, giving him a black eye. Josef had no visible injuries except for a bloody nose."

"Whoa," Serena whispered. "Did they see you?"

"Only Josef. He glanced down the staircase and saw me at the bottom. The next morning, I was called into the director's office and asked about the incident. Josef stared at me with such hope and trust in his eyes, yet I lied. I told the director I saw nothing. I wanted to compete against Hans and win. That boy had hurt my pride, and I had something to prove."

"Did you win?" Serena asked.

"No, and the school expelled Josef. I never expected that to happen." Max placed both hands on the table. "Now, do you see why it doesn't matter? We cannot reverse time so I can tell the true story. Would Josef have become the soloist? Or would Hans still become one of the most recognized singers of our day?"

"That Hans?" Serena blinked several times.

"Yes. Now do you understand why Josef must let go of this? This happened over forty years ago. Who would he tell? A tabloid? A social media site? Would people take sides? They'd attack Josef, this unknown man, who appears jealous of Hans and wishes to cause trouble for him. Josef wants me to tell the world, but what is the point? He could get hurt all over again."

"You're doing this to protect Josef?" Jack asked.

"In a way, but shouldn't we leave it alone?" Max gave Serena a pleading look.

"I can't say." Serena lifted her shoulder. "This is tough. You may be right, let it be."

"Our choir director passed away ten years ago. I cannot go to him and say I was a foolish young boy who lied about Josef. No one at the school may even remember Josef or me."

"You feel it's best to let this go," Serena said.

"Exactly," Max answered. "But Josef does not agree. He will hold a grudge against me to the end of time, and I fear it may escalate now that we have crossed paths again."

"I hope not," Serena replied, resting her chin on her hand. "I certainly hope not."

* * * *

Serena readied the table for the next day and slipped the Human Resource notebook into her handbag. She didn't want to stay a minute longer than necessary since she wanted to join Jack at the stakeout. "Five minutes to go," she mumbled.

"This is important, girls," a voice said from the doorway.

Serena recognized her cousin's tone and glanced toward the sound. *I swear she has a French accent.* With a forced smile, she asked, "How can I assist you, Sasha?"

"These two." Sasha pushed Anna and Sophie forward. "Have something to show you."

"No, please don't make us," Sophie whined. "I want to keep him."

"So do I," Anna said, holding her nutcracker tight to her chest. "They were gifts from him."

"From who?" Serena asked.

"The Nutcracker Bandit," Sophie said with a giggle.

Where did they hear that? I only told Jack. "Did he present them to you?" Serena stared at the girls as only a mother could.

"No." Sophie hung her head.

"We found them on the stage," Anna answered. "Right on the spots where we stand."

"Do you have proof the bandit is male?" Serena closed one eye.

"I…don't…I…just assumed," Anna stammered.

"Hand them over." Serena grabbed two bags and popped them open. "Place them in here, please." She labeled the nutcrackers and set them on the chair next to her. "Did you see anything, Sasha?" She looked at her cousin.

"No. I walked by the stage after the girls found the nutcrackers. How could I not notice? They squealed in delight and danced around the stage with those things." Sasha pointed to the bagged nutcrackers and pulled back as if they gave off a bad smell. "I told them to report their findings to you. When I checked on them now, they still had them in their possession. Or should I say, they hid them, so I'd assume they reported to you. I saw the top of one behind a bookbag, confronted the girls and brought them here."

"How could we give them up?" Anna asked. "The Nutcracker bandit chose those specifically for us. Look at them. They are drummers. We're not drummers but love music."

"I see." Serena noticed both nutcrackers held drums. One sported dark hair paired with a matching straight mustache, while the other had white hair. They wore uniforms of black hats, red jackets and white pants. "Sorry, girls, they're evidence."

"Evidence?" Anna seemed annoyed. "He or she has done nothing wrong. It's added some needed fun for the market participants."

"I see your point," Serena replied. "But we must treat this as suspicious until we learn otherwise. You may go. But remember, I know where to find you."

After the girls exited the tearoom, Sasha turned to Serena. "You were great! I almost believed those threats. You sounded like an actual cop." She lowered her voice and repeated what Serena had said. "You may go. But remember, I know where to find you."

"This isn't funny, Sasha. Some people think the nutcrackers are threats."

"Okay." Sasha pointed to the chair across from Serena. "Mind if I sit?"

"Will you still sit if I say no?"

Sasha slid into the seat. "Serena, I haven't seen you since the breakfast incident."

"Is that what we're calling it? It wasn't a date?"

"No. Justice and I saw each other in the lobby. He asked if I'd eaten breakfast. When I said no, he asked me to join him in the restaurant. What was I supposed to do? Text you and ask permission?"

"You're a grown woman, Sasha. I wouldn't tell you what to do, but I'd hope you would have enough sense not to date my ex."

"I'm sorry. As soon as I sat down, I knew I should have texted. Before I got the chance, you were standing at our table." Sasha let out a breath. "So, I'm telling you now that I agreed to have drinks with Justice tonight."

"Did he tell you he has a girlfriend?" Serena asked.

"Does he?"

"I'm not sure, but you better ask him. Justice proposed to me last winter but admitted to having a girlfriend when I asked."

"That dog."

"Just be careful."

"I will. It's just drinks."

"That's what they all say." Serena pursed her lips.

"Forgiven?" Sasha slid her hand across the table. "Can we be friends again?"

"Friends." Serena placed her hand on top of Sasha's. "I have bigger things to focus on than Justice. It appears whoever comes into this room to file a complaint or is a witness gets a nutcracker. Someone is watching, and I can't figure out how."

"Do you want my opinion?" Sasha grimaced.

"Yes, any point of view is valuable."

"The culprit always has market access. They have the option to enter the storeroom, mingle with the crowds or return late at night."

"Excellent observation," Serena said in a sarcastic tone. "As if we hadn't thought of that."

"And it's a man," Sasha replied, wrinkling her nose at Serena.

"What led you to that conclusion?" Serena asked, now interested in her cousin's train of thought.

"Think, Serena." Sasha tapped her temple. "Would a woman steal a box of nutcrackers and use them to threaten people?"

"Maybe?" Serena lifted her shoulders.

"I never would. I'd confront them face to face."

"You would, Sasha, but not everyone. People often hide their identities on social media to attack from a safe distance."

Sasha gestured to the nutcrackers lying on the chair. "The girls planned to tell me they turned in the nutcrackers, but after I found the first one, they confessed they hadn't seen you. I discovered the second nutcracker hidden behind the stage. When I picked it up, I caught a slight scent of a man's cologne. I can't place it, but I am sure of the smell."

"Anyone we know?" Serena arched a brow.

"No, but it's advertised as a man's cologne."

"Why didn't you lead with that story?" Serena opened one bag and sniffed. "You're right. I can barely smell it, but it reminds me of a man's cologne."

Chapter Thirteen

Friday morning Serena met Mia and Lily at the tearoom. "I have an hour before the shops open," she announced as she took her seat.

"We miss these breakfast meetings," Mia cried. "We've hardly seen you since the market began."

"At least she texts us," Lily said. "After receiving your last one Wednesday night, I've tried to sniff out the culprit." She giggled. "I did my best to get close to Josef and Max to see if they were wearing cologne. Trust me, it wasn't easy."

"Do they?" Serena asked.

"Yes, both do."

"You must visit security and find the nutcracker drummers," Serena said. "See if they are a match."

"You mean sniff them out?" Lily asked with a huge grin.

"Yes," Serena chuckled. "You catch my drift."

"Of cologne?" Lily tapped the table as she giggled.

"Will you two stop it?" Mia said. "It's not as serious as the others, but this case has the potential to turn deadly."

"Don't say that." Serena placed her palms together and gazed up at the ceiling. "We've gotten through a week with no major mishaps."

"It's great news, and let's hope it continues," Mia replied. "Tell us what happened on your stakeout with Jack."

"Nothing." Serena dropped her shoulders. "Josef cleaned up his shop, took his leftover goods to the storeroom and went to dinner. Jack and I ate, too, so we could watch him. When he finished, Josef went to his room."

"Ugh." Lily dropped her head. "You learned nothing. Will you try again?"

"We might," Serena said. "Jack has people checking the security footage. They'll find something."

Jun arrived at the table with teapots, cups and scones. Serena loved a scone with lemon curd and clotted cream, and Jun always added extra to the serving bowls. She poured oolong tea into Serena's cup and said, "Enjoy." She started to turn but instead faced Serena. "How is Eve doing?"

"The new server?" Serena asked.

"Yes. When you sit up front, you are in her station."

"She's great, Jun, but I miss you." Serena patted her arm.

Jun bowed her head. "Thank you for saying that." She smiled as she turned to serve Lily her tea.

"And no one can replace you, Jun," Serena added. "I just want you to know."

After she left, Lily said, "I hope Jun isn't jealous. She loves you, Serena, and sees Eve enjoying your company instead of her."

"No one can replace Jun," Serena said. "I'll make sure she is aware of that fact." She added some sugar to her tea. "I sent you a list of victims and nutcrackers they received. Have you had the chance to study it?"

"Should we include Sasha's ballerina in that list?" Mia asked.

"I'm not sure," Serena answered. "Josef gifted her the nutcracker, *but* he placed it in her shop when she wasn't there. We should include the second one she found and mark it as suspicious."

"We should examine what these people have in common, and it may lead to the guilty party," Lily stated.

"They angered someone," Mia said.

"There's more to it," Lily replied. "We initially labeled this as a prank, but it's gone beyond that. Someone is sending a message. It's personal."

"Or this person is trying to frame someone," Mia answered. "Like Josef. He may be innocent but sure looks guilty. Is someone out to get him? Who are the suspects, Serena? Have you started your murder board?"

"Since there's been no murder, I haven't, but I need to go to my office and start one."

"You haven't gone to your office since the Merry and Bright Christmas Market opened." Mia took a sip of tea. "You're usually there on weekdays and sometimes weekends working on your next book."

"I've barely had time to go to my office," Serena answered. "Although, *Secrets, Suspicions, and Stolen Pearls* is almost complete."

"I can't wait." Lily rubbed her hands together. "Is Linda the killer? I assume you're basing the story on what happened last summer."

"Lily, I don't use actual names, and the release date is spring. I can't give away the plot."

Lily stuck out her lower lip.

"Fine." Serena released a loud breath. "Yes, I based it on last summer's events, and Linda is the killer…although I named her Lynette."

"I won't tell." Lily made a zipping motion across her mouth. "Knowing you, you're working on an outline for the next book after *Secrets*."

"I bet not," Mia said. "Serena needs a real-life experience to motivate her. But…" She gestured toward the gardens. "A lot is happening right out there. You can invent a murder."

"People love to read holiday-themed books, Serena," Lily said. "I've read many novels that have Christmas as the focal point."

Serena held up her hand. "Thanks for the input. You are great supporters of my books, but let's focus on one thing at a time. Can we get back to the nutcrackers? I'd like to discover the person responsible and end it today."

"Mom?"

Serena glanced over her shoulder. "I'm here, Jade." She rose quickly from her seat when she saw her daughter's panicked expression. Serena grasped onto Jade's hands. "Your hands are shaking. What's wrong?"

"Can you come with me?" Jade's voice stirred with emotion.

"We'll all come," Lily said, rising from her seat.

"I don't want to make a scene," Jade replied, her voice barely a whisper. "Please, follow me."

Serena checked to see if her friends followed as they wound their way through the gardens and into an unused cul-de-sac area off the main walkway. Jade stopped before reaching the end. "This." She pointed toward the landscape.

Lily grasped Serena's arm. "Do you see what I see?"

"Yes," Serena whispered.

A pair of legs, dressed in red and white striped stockings and green felt shoes which curled at the toes, protruded from the garden landscape. The person lay face down in the imitation snow used to decorate around the plants. The fluffy substance around his head appeared to be dyed red. Yet, this wasn't a holiday scene gone wrong. *It's blood.* Serena took a step closer. She noticed an object embedded in the back of Carmody's head. "A court jester," she whispered.

"Is that a nutcracker?" Mia asked in a quiet voice. "We need to call nine-one-one. Get an ambulance here." She searched for her cell, digging in her bag. "I'll alert grandmother."

"I'll call security." Lily let go of Serena's arm. "And Jack."

A piercing scream came from behind Serena. The sound penetrated through her bones, and she identified the person without having to turn. Serena knew it was Jewel. "Someone get her out of here," she cried.

"I've got her, Serena," Justice's voice rose over their daughter's screams. "Do what you need to do."

Unable to move, Serena felt as if she was in a trance. She stared at the blood pooling around Carmody's head and longed to remove the nutcracker lodged in his skull. "Who would do something like this?" she whispered.

"Someone who is desperate," Jack said, wrapping his hands around Serena's shoulders.

"Jack." Serena leaned against him, letting out her breath. "Is Jewel still here? I can't look."

"No, Justice took Jade and Jewel to your room. Emergency personnel just pulled up to the hotel, but we must move so the police can document the crime scene before they remove the body. Are you able to walk?"

"Yes, please take me to my office. I need to stop shaking before I go upstairs to see the girls."

On their way out of the secluded corner, Serena and Jack almost collided with Detective Bill Mitchell. The short, heavy-set officer with tufts of brown hair on either side of his balding head made a disapproving noise. "I should have guessed," he said.

"Guessed what, Bill?" Jack asked.

"That you two would be involved." Bill gestured to Serena. "Has she solved the case yet?"

"Bill." Jack's face hardened, and his jaw twitched. "The young man was her daughter's boyfriend. This is personal."

"Oh. I'm sorry for your loss." Bill tried to sound sorry, yet Serena doubted he was.

"Loss? Is he dead?" Serena sniffed.

"I haven't seen the body, but someone called in a murder," Bill answered. "If you'll excuse me."

Jack guided Serena away from the scene and through the gardens. From the corner of her eye, she caught Samurai leaping from the water. *Does he want to tell me something*?

Police officers blocked the garden's entryway and stepped aside for Jack and Serena. Nina stood in the lobby, appearing distraught. As the couple approached her, Nina cocked her head toward the office hallway. "We can speak more freely there," she said.

They walked in silence until they reached the hall, and the throngs of people had subsided. "What is your plan for the market?" Serena asked.

"I want your opinion, Serena. I'm conflicted. If we shut down, the girls' project will be a failure. It is close to opening time, and I need to decide."

"It doesn't just affect the girls," Serena said. "The vendors are counting on one more week of sales."

"If they've removed the body, the police will tape off the crime scene. It's in an inconspicuous place," Jack replied. "Maybe Randi can find some decorations to block the path, and the market can open."

"That sounds cold," Nina said. "We are disrespecting the dead."

Serena knew how important tradition was to Nina, yet she ran a five-star hotel. "It will scare the guests if they hear someone was murdered in the gardens…" She shuddered.

"It's likely a market participant with a grudge against another one," Jack said. "There isn't some random person roaming the gardens with a nutcracker, looking to bludgeon guests."

"True, but we cannot publicize that. I will ask the gingerbread people to distribute flyers stating the market is closed and will reopen tomorrow at the regular time," Nina announced. "It will give the police time to do their job and our staff to clean up the area."

"Shall we place a candle or create a small shrine for Carmody?" Serena asked. "The vendors can visit when the police give the all-clear and pay their respects."

"No matter how you see it, there is no right answer," Nina said, hanging her head. "It won't remain a secret for long. Word will get out."

"Get your people on it now," Serena said, pointing toward Nina's office. "Jack and I will be in my office if you need us."

"Thank you." Nina took Serena's hand in hers and squeezed before heading down the hallway.

"Serena?" Jack wrinkled his brow as he gestured toward her office. "Don't you always lock your door?"

"Yes." Serena noticed her door was ajar. "That's strange."

"Can you manage for a few minutes?" Jack asked. "I want to go down to security." He opened the door the rest of the way. "After I check your office."

Serena noticed her chair wasn't tucked under her light-oak desk but couldn't recall how she had left it. She sank into the white padded seat and recalled the day she asked the girls to help her redecorate the place.

"I'd love to redo this space with something bold and daring," Jade had said. Her eyes flashed with excitement.

"But that's not Mom, Jade. She needs a soft touch, too," Jewel had replied.

Serena remembered saying, "See? You're the perfect duo for the job. Bold and soft."

"My two girls," Serena whispered. "The sensitive one had her heart ripped from her chest today. She didn't deserve it." She spun in the chair, taking in the décor. Navy blue walls with white trim surrounded her. A golden elephant, giraffe and tiger sat among gold-framed family photos on the white floating shelves. Her favorite was the gold geometric lamp the girls had hung in the middle of the room.

Serena slowly spun in her chair, gazing at the ceiling, then down at the floor. As she passed the floating shelves again, Serena slammed her feet to the floor to bring the chair to a stop. She blinked to make sure she wasn't seeing things. There on one shelf, standing tall and proud, was a nutcracker.

* * * *

Jack burst in, shouting to Serena, "You won't believe this…" Their eyes met, and she knew he saw the fear and confusion. "What's wrong?"

Serena pointed to the shelf with the recently placed nutcracker, dressed in green with a cuckoo clock hanging from his belt. "That. Does it mean my time is up?"

Jack walked to the shelf and raised his arm to measure the distance. "No, but it gives us a clue. The suspect needs to be tall to reach this shelf. I doubt anyone had time to stand on a chair." He dug into his back pocket and produced a latex glove. "Don't touch it until I can get a bag," he said, resting the nutcracker on her desk.

"Do you think Carmody put it on the shelf?" Serena asked. "Someone saw him and confronted him. Not wanting to leave evidence behind, Carmody retrieved the jester he planned to give to his next victim, and this person ripped it away from him. Carmody ran, and the suspect chased him, using the nutcracker as a weapon."

"That is one theory," Jack replied. "But it doesn't make Carmody a killer, does it? He is the victim. In your scenario, he was using the nutcrackers to pull harmless pranks. Someone caught him in the act. Who is the only person who would become angry at the sight of Carmody with the nutcrackers?"

"Josef," Serena whispered. *The angry cinnamon bear.* She pictured the animal, exposing its teeth and claws, ready to pounce.

"I've got to make a phone call, Serena." Jack stepped outside her office.

When he returned, Serena said in a sad voice, "You had him arrested." She stared at her hands folded on the desk. "It all makes sense now. Josef wasn't the nutcracker bandit. Carm was. Harmless fun turned into a deadly confrontation."

Chapter Fourteen

"I have more evidence," Jack said. "Mind if I sit at your desk?" He held up a flash drive.

"You found something." Serena rose and offered her chair.

Jack popped the drive into a computer slot and sat down. "These people visited your office every night after the market closed."

"These people?" Serena leaned over the chair to watch the video. "Is that Jade?"

Her daughter stood in the hall outside Serena's office. She glanced in both directions, then waved to someone out of sight before unlocking the door.

"I never gave her a key," Serena said.

"She gave a very convincing argument to the front desk," Jack replied. "I stopped there before coming here. According to the staff, you granted Jade permission to use your office during the market." He tapped the screen. "All this happened after market hours."

Serena watched Andre, Jewel and Carmody enter her office as Jade closed the door behind them. "My office became a love nest," she wailed.

"Maybe not," Jack offered. "Perhaps they needed some peace after a busy day at the market. There's more." He backed out of the footage and clicked on a different folder. "This took place another night."

Serena watched as her daughters and their two boyfriends went into her office, followed by Sophie, Leo, Anna and Felix. "It's turned into a lovefest," she cried. "Sophie acted as if she liked Leo, but Anna rolled her eyes when she mentioned Leo, Alex and Felix. What is she doing with Felix?"

"Serena." Jack got up and led her to the navy and white canopy-striped sofa on the far wall. "Sit and take a few deep breaths. We can't focus on personal relationships now. Our priority is the task at hand. Every person who entered this office is under suspicion. One of them left your door ajar so they could return."

A knock came at the door, and Lily peeked through a small opening she had created. "Is it okay to come in?"

"Yes, please," Serena said. "You saw the footage?"

"I did." Lily sat in a chair next to the sofa. "This may answer what happened to Carmody." She revealed another flash drive she held in the palm of her hand.

The trio gathered around Serena's computer and waited while Lily retrieved the footage. "There are no cameras in your office, Serena. As you know, we only place them in public areas of the hotel. Watch as Carmody approaches the office door. He's empty-handed." Lily pointed to his hands. "He notices the door is ajar, looks inside and appears to be having a conversation with someone. Carm backs away from the door, turns and runs. Someone dressed exactly like Carmody, except for the jester mask and gloves, gives chase." She paused and gazed up at Jack and Serena. "Can you see what the elf is holding?"

"A court jester nutcracker," Serena whispered. "Who is the person wearing an elf costume?" She faced Jack. "Any ideas?"

"We have a body type now, and from the shape, I'd guess the person is male. It's not Josef or Max. I believe it's someone younger. Does Carmody have any adversaries?"

"Jewel said he likes to work alone and shunned the gingerbread people, preferring to do his own act. The choir seems to enjoy his antics but perhaps some don't. We need to interview them, Jack."

Lily switched to another feed. "Look. Carmody stopped inside the gardens, turned as if he had decided to reason with this person. It looks like he was on his way to tell you, Serena, and used it as a threat to make the elf retreat. Instead, the masked one pushes Carmody in the chest, and Carm runs into the vacant cul-de-sac. Don't ask me why."

"Perhaps he got disoriented?" Serena watched as the masked elf trailed Carmody into a secluded area and strike him from behind with the nutcracker. Carmody fell face first into the landscape, and the person ran from the scene. "How could he be so cruel?" She shook her head. "He left him for dead."

"Or he panicked," Jack said. "Remember, if this masked elf is young, he didn't think it through and ran."

"He never checked to see if Carmody was still breathing and left him for dead," Serena cried. "Jack, call your contact at the station and see if you can get any information. We're assuming Carmody died, but is he?"

"You mean call Sue?" Jack smirked.

"Yes, Sue."

Sue Downing worked in forensics and had worked on other cases with Jack. Serena had met her when she helped with the model murder case. She and Jack appeared close, and Serena had been a bit jealous. Since then, she learned Jack considered her a friend and valued her opinion. He had no romantic feelings for her.

"I'll speak with her," Jack said, "But first I need to call Bill Mitchell and report what we found on the security footage. He needs to release Josef. I don't believe he's the man in the elf suit." He took Serena's hand. "Go see your girls. I need to discuss this with Nina before I head to the police station. And Lily?"

"Yes?" Lily looked up from the computer screen.

"Please inform security to check footage starting from day one of the market and look for a masked elf. This person chose an excellent disguise. One would assume it was Carmody and not pay close attention."

"Okay, and I'll help look," Lily said. She rose from the chair and hugged Serena. "We'll find who did this."

"Thank you." Serena soaked in her friend's empathy. "If you find anything…"

"I'll text you," Lily said.

"When I return, Serena and I will start the interviews." Jack faced Serena. "Bill won't be far behind once he views the footage."

"In other words, we need to do this quickly before he arrives." Serena nodded and took a deep breath. "I'll stay in my suite until I hear from you."

* * * *

Serena opened the door to her suite and found Justice watching TV, although she doubted he was awake. His chin almost touched his chest. "What are you doing?" she hissed.

"Serena!" Justice jumped from the sofa. "What are you doing here?"

"I live here," Serena said in a sarcastic voice.

"Sorry. I forgot where I was for a minute. I must have dozed off."

"Typical," Serena mumbled.

"What did you say?"

"How are the girls?"

"They are in your bedroom." Justice gestured down the hallway. "Once we got Jewel calmed down, Jade volunteered to sit with her and said I should come out here. Jewel didn't want her daddy, Serena. She needs you."

Serena was glad to hear Justice say those words in a nonjudgmental tone. He sank back into the couch and covered his face with his hand. "Did you discover anything?"

"Yes, there is security footage." Serena described what she had seen.

"Sounds like a prank gone bad. Stupid kid."

"We were stupid kids once, Justice."

"But we didn't commit murder."

"Did you say murder?" Jewel stood in the hallway with Jade, hand over her heart.

Serena opened her arms, and Jewel rushed into them. "I'm so sorry, baby." She kissed the top of Jewel's head.

Justice had gotten up from the sofa and joined the hug. "I didn't mean for you to hear that, baby girl. There is still no news on Carmody's condition."

"I heard mom's voice, and I wanted to see her." Jewel sniffed.

"Did you hear everything?" Serena asked.

"Most." Jewel stepped away from Serena but still held her hand.

"Let's sit." Serena motioned to the sofa.

Justice sat on one side of Jewel, Serena on the other. Serena repeated what she learned in her office and asked the girls not to relay any information to their friends.

"We won't, Mom," Jade said.

"Even Andre?" Serena arched a brow.

"I can't keep anything from you, can I?" Jade lifted the corner of her mouth. "I won't tell Andre."

"We'll discuss how you snuck into my office another time, Ms. Jade Tate," Serena said in a strict voice.

Jade hung her head. "Sorry. If I hadn't, Carm might be…"

"No." Serena shook her head. "Do not blame yourself."

"How could any of our friends do this to Carmody?" Jewel wailed. "Once I discover who did this, they'll be sorry. I'll take a nutcracker to their…"

"Shh," Serena whispered. "Enough. Let's wait to hear from Jack. Hopefully, he'll have new information. When he returns to the hotel, we're going to interview your friends."

A knock at the door interrupted their conversation. "I'll get it," Jade said. When she opened the door, Nina and Mia stood in the hall.

"Come in." Serena motioned to them.

"How is our little one?" Nina asked in a nurturing voice. She petted Jewel's arm and whispered, "We will take care of this, sweetheart, don't you worry."

Justice cleared his throat. "Jewel was just telling us how she'd use a nutcracker on the…"

"Justice! Where are your manners?" Serena widened her eyes. "Please, sit," she said to Mia and Nina.

"We've come to offer our help," Mia said. "Grandmother has a wonderful idea after speaking with Jack." She turned to face Jade. "We want you to invite the choir and the gingerbread people to the tearoom. Tell them you're holding a vigil for Carmody. We will supply the drinks and food, buffet-style. It will appear casual but will give your mom and Jack time to question people."

"Okay," Jade answered. "I'm in. What time should I tell everyone?"

"Four p.m. It gives the staff three hours to prepare," Mia replied.

Serena's phone rang, and she checked the screen. "It's Jack." She got up and headed into the hallway. "Jack?"

"Serena," Jack said in a solemn voice. "It's not good news. Sue heard that Carmody was pronounced dead at the hospital."

"What?" Serena gasped and everyone in the suite made eye contact with her. "I'm sorry to hear. Are you coming back now?"

"Yes, I can't do any more at the station. The fingerprint results from all the nutcrackers are in, but since the elf wore gloves, it's not surprising they didn't find their prints."

"I need to break the news to Jewel," Serena whispered. "I'll meet you in my office in a few minutes." She ended the call and looked at Jewel's anxious face. "I'm so sorry, honey. He…Carmody didn't make it."

"What? No!" Jewel threw her body against Justice and sobbed.

Justice wrapped his arms around her, whispering into her hair. Serena blinked back tears as she watched father console daughter. Her heart ached for Jewel, but realized no words would help at this moment. As a mother, she felt powerless to protect her from the evils of the world.

Sitting up, Jewel pointed at the door. "Mom, go. Find out who did this. Don't come back until you do."

Serena hurried toward her daughter, and Jewel stood and clung to her. "I'll do whatever you need, Jewel. I'll stay as long as you want."

"Why? To watch me cry? I'd rather have you catch a killer."

Serena stepped back and gazed into her daughter's eyes. "You really mean that, don't you?"

"I do. How many times must Jade and I tell you? We are proud of you, Mom. You're one badass woman. When I grow up, I want to be just like you."

Tears streamed down Serena's cheeks. She felt Jewel's arms go around her, and then another pair. "I can stay and help them get ready for later," Mia said. "Girls, you've got to put on a show to help your mom. Can you do that?"

"Yes," they said in unison.

"I love you," Serena said. "All of you in this room." Then she amended, "Except you, Justice. You're on the 'just okay' list."

"I'll take whatever I can get, Serena." Justice chuckled. "Now do what Jewel asked. Go catch the killer."

* * * *

Serena unlocked her office door and headed straight for her murder board. She unpinned the scarf and stared at the blank space. "Does my daughter's social circle contain a killer?" Serena closed her eyes. "No, it must be a mistake. None of those young people are killers. Still. Someone is dead."

Walking toward her desk, Serena planned to find pictures on social media sites. After obtaining Carmody's photo, she printed the young men from the choir and the gingerbread people. As she labeled the last photo, Jack walked through the open door.

"Hey, Serena." Jack ran his hand through his hair. "How did it come to this? We swore we wouldn't let it happen again."

"Jack." Serena slipped her arms around his neck and kissed him. "What's the saying? Never say never."

"So true." Jack sighed, returning the kiss. "How's Jewel?"

"Upset. Sad, but doing her best to hang in there. She ordered me to find the killer."

"Did she?" Jack's lips twitched. "That's our girl."

"Aww, Jack, you are so sweet. I'm glad you care about her."

"Why wouldn't I? They're your kids, Serena. How could I not?"

"Some men wouldn't, Jack Ando, and you know it." Serena kissed him again. "I finished the board. Let's study it and play motive, means and opportunity. It's the best way to eliminate a few suspects."

"I can save you time," Sunita said, leaning on the doorframe, appearing pale and out of breath. "I know who did it." She struggled to walk into the room. "What's wrong with me?" Her hand flew to her forehead. "I feel dizzy. Tired."

Sunita took another step and crumpled to the floor.

"Sunita!" Serena yelled. "Jack, check to see if she is okay."

Chapter Fifteen

Jack placed two fingers against Sunita's neck.

"Well?" Serena asked in a shaky voice.

"She's got a pulse," Jack answered. "Did you call nine-one-one?"

"Yes, and alerted security. They'll meet the ambulance at the entrance and escort them here. Nina is on her way down from my suite. She will want a full report."

"You didn't waste time. Great job," Jack said as he stood and stepped away from Sunita. "Don't touch anything, Serena. Stay where you are."

"Sunita was about to tell us who killed Carmody," Serena said, her voice shaking. "Did the same person do this to her?"

"Maybe?" Jack grimaced. "A doctor needs to see her before we make any assumptions. She may have become dehydrated from too much dancing and not drinking enough liquids."

Serena bit back a smile as she pictured Sunita dancing with such enthusiasm she passed out from exhaustion. "If so, shouldn't she have regained consciousness by now?"

A noise in the hallway made them turn toward the door. A paramedic walked in backwards, guiding a stretcher into the room. Jack and Serena moved to the back of the office to get out of their way. Bill Mitchell strolled in after the second paramedic cleared the entryway.

"What have we here?" Bill folded his hands over his rounded belly. "Another murder? Right here in your office, Ms. Tate."

"Bill." Jack's voice sounded deadly. "Ms. Patel is alive."

"That's good news, but that doesn't help the boy, does it?" Bill said as he pointed at the couple. "Before I leave for the hospital, I have a few questions about the victim."

The medics pushed Sunita, now lying on the stretcher, from the room. Jack and Serena took seats on the sofa and stared up at Bill.

"Tell me everything." Bill paced in front of them. "One at a time, of course."

Jack and Serena's stories matched, and when Bill appeared satisfied, he bid them a good day.

"Did he tell us to have a nice day?" Serena wrinkled her brow.

"He sure did." Jack shook his head.

"I waited until Detective Mitchell left," Nina said, knocking on the open door. "How is Sunita?"

"Alive," Jack answered. "I'm going to call Sue and see if she can get her hands on the tox screening and doctor's report." He stood and produced his phone. "Please, Nina, sit." He offered his spot and walked into the hallway.

Nina slid in next to Serena and took her hand. "How are you holding up?"

"Not well." Serena dropped her head. "I want to visit Samurai, Nina, but things keep going sideways."

"You want to discuss things with him," Nina said. "I understand."

"Sam might have seen something, Nina. What is your opinion?"

"Anything is possible. Take a detour on your way to the tearoom, Serena. Samurai will enjoy the visit, and it will give you time to think. Jade has invited the university students to attend Carmody's memorial, and they all gave positive responses."

"I heard the police asked the vendors and entertainers to stay at the hotel. Where are you putting them?"

"We opened the bridal room and the banquet hall. There's plenty of room."

"I'm sorry this happened," Serena groaned. "The Christmas market was growing in popularity and turning a profit."

"Don't worry about those things, Serena. People matter. The rest will work itself out." Nina patted Serena's hand.

"Now that Josef and Max are cleared, who do you suspect?" Serena asked.

Nina answered without hesitation, "Anna Wagner."

Her answer surprised Serena. "We were leaning towards a male suspect."

"Anna is tall and lean and could flatten her bosom," Nina said. "She seems like the jealous type. We don't know

Carmody and Anna's history. Perhaps they dated? He moved on, and she didn't."

"We only focused on revenge, but jealousy is a motive," Serena replied. "With so many young adults here, it's bound to happen. I never thought of that angle. Nina, you are a genius." She motioned at her wall. "Let's look at my board."

Nina joined Serena to study the murder board. "You only have men on it, Serena," she said.

"I'll add Anna." Serena strode to her computer, found a photo and hit the print button.

"Let's try to eliminate a few candidates," Nina said. She touched two pictures. "What about them?"

"Jacob and Brandon. They're part of the gingerbread team. If I recall, Jade mentioned they had significant others and would leave as soon as the market closed for the day."

"Enough reason to remove them from the board."

Serena and Nina debated each contender, discussing each person's possible motive, means and opportunity. When Jack returned from making his calls, they had cleared most of the suspects.

Serena stepped back to admire their work. "What do you think?" she asked him.

"You added a female," Jack grimaced.

"Nina's idea. She feels Anna has a jealous streak, which gave us an additional motive."

"Jealousy," Jack replied. "But does she fit the physical profile?"

"She's tall," Serena answered. "About five foot ten."

"I'd guess Carmody is about six-one," Jack replied.

"Close enough." Serena looked at him to see if he agreed.

"Let me view the rest," Jack said, stepping towards the board. "Besides Anna, you've got Andre, Leo and Felix up there. You're sure about these three?"

"No, but it's a start. After we conduct our interviews, we may add or subtract," Serena answered.

"Jack, did you speak with Sue?" Nina asked.

"She'll text me as soon as she gets the report," Jack answered. "I need to go to the security office and check on things. Is that okay, Serena? It's getting close to teatime, and I promised to be there."

"It's fine. I also have something to do before I go to the restaurant. I'll meet you at the tearoom."

"I'll walk with you," Nina said, linking arms with Serena.

The three parted ways when they reached the lobby. Serena and Nina headed for the red Torii gate and Jack to the elevators. A chain blocked the entrance, bearing a sign that read, "Closed for repairs."

"Your staff came up with a great idea," Serena said, gesturing to the sign.

"For now." Nina sighed as she unlocked the chain and let Serena into the gardens. "I hope we get a full report from the police so we can release a statement with concrete facts. I do not want rumors to spread." Nina stopped at the fence surrounding the pond. "This is my best thinking spot, Serena."

"Mine, too." Serena placed her hands on the railing. Within a minute, Samurai popped to the surface. "Hey, Sam. I'm glad to see you. It's been a long day."

The koi stared at her as if he understood. He swam in a few circles and surfaced even closer to her.

"I'll leave you two to talk," Nina said. "Samurai, it's been a pleasure."

If Samurai could speak, Serena swore he said, "Start asking questions." She felt a connection to the red and white koi she couldn't explain to anyone. Samurai understood her pain and would try to help. "Ready for yes and no questions?" she asked him.

Sam disappeared underwater, and Serena dug in her bag for his treats. "I've got honey oat cereal." She shook the bag. "That's strange. Samurai always comes up for food. Maybe he doesn't want to answer questions. It's okay, Sam. We'll just visit." She paused in thought. "Wait a minute. You didn't see anything, did you?"

The fish sprung into the air, causing droplets of water to fall on Serena. After a deep dive, his red head emerged from the pond.

"Here you go," Serena said, tossing the cereal into his open mouth. "The killer was in disguise, Sam. You probably saw him chasing Carmody earlier today but have no clue who it was. We don't either. But don't worry, Jack and I are on the case."

Serena summarized the events of the day, ending with the new motive, jealousy. "You seem to agree, Sam." She sprinkled the rest of the cereal into the water. "For you and your friends."

"Hey, Sissy," Sasha said from behind her. "Who are you talking to?"

"Myself." Serena turned away from the pond.

"I heard about Sunita. Is she okay?" Sasha pointed to a bench. "Mind if we sit?"

"I only have a few minutes," Serena replied. "I'm on my way to the tearoom."

"For Carmody's memorial?"

"You heard."

"It's a great idea for the college kids to mourn together," Sasha said. "Keeps them busy, too. It's been a long, boring day for everyone. Sorry, I didn't mean it like that. We are praying for Sunita and Carmody, of course."

"You've been in the reception hall?" Serena asked.

"Yeah, it gives me something to do since the market isn't open. I don't want to sit in my room and stare at the walls."

"Did you see Sunita earlier?"

"Yes, I was sitting at a table with her. She offered to get us iced teas from the drink table."

A warning sounded in Serena's head. "From a pitcher?"

"Yes. She poured two glasses of tea from a pitcher. Why?"

"You saw her pour the tea."

"Serena, you're scaring me. Why all the questions?" Sasha widened her eyes.

"Please, just answer. I'll explain later. Did Sunita immediately return to the table with the drinks?" Serena's heart raced. *Was this another prank gone wrong or something more sinister? Did someone tamper with the tea?* "How do you feel, Sasha?"

"I'm fine, and to answer your question, a dancer approached Sunita, and she set the drinks down to speak with her."

"How many people were at the table?"

"A lot. Nina and her staff provided a wonderful buffet for us, and as you know, people love free food and drink." Sasha chuckled. "Max insisted his choir help with chores since the hotel so generously provided them with food and drink. A staff member suggested they work at the drink table. The kids delivered water pitchers to tables, refilled tea, coffee and lemonade on the main one and returned empty glasses to the kitchen."

"I'm glad to hear people are showing their appreciation," Serena said. "Now, what about Sunita? How long was she at the table?"

"I'm not a stalker, Serena. I didn't watch her every move. I believe I answered texts until she came back with the drinks." Sasha paused and tapped her chin. "No, wait. She left our tea on the table, and someone brought the glasses to us." Sasha held up her hand. "Don't ask. I forget who it was. Sunita apologized and said she had so much on her mind she'd forgotten them."

"So much on her mind," Serena mumbled. "She planned to come to my office and tell me who killed Carmody."

"No!" Sasha leaned back against the bench. "She never said a word to me. Who did it?"

"Sunita fainted before she got the chance to tell."

"I hope she's okay," Sasha said. "I like her." She placed her hand on Serena's arm. "Thanks for urging me to come. I've had a great time. Mom and Dad plan to drive in from Vegas, attend the market's close, and stay for Christmas. You don't mind having us all at your house for the holiday?"

Tears welled in Serena's eyes. "Not at all. You've given me the best present a girl could ask for, Sasha."

"Will the market reopen?" Sasha whispered. "Not the merriest of Christmases that I had imagined."

"We can't make that decision until we get more answers," Serena replied. "But I *am* going to get them. After Jade and Jewel's memorial for Carmody, I'm going to the hospital to see Sunita."

"If she's awake, give her my best," Sasha said.

* * * *

Jade waved to Serena as she entered the tearoom. "Over here, Mom."

Serena greeted people as she walked through the restaurant to reach her daughter. Jade stood with Andre, who Serena thought looked more like a member of the football team than a theater major. She made the snap decision to interview him first. "Where's Jewel?" Serena checked the surrounding area.

"She's with Anna and Sophie," Jade answered.

"Hello, Ms. Tate," Andre said, giving her a killer grin that reminded her of Justice.

"Hi." Serena slipped her arm through his and looked at Jade. "Mind if I borrow him for a minute?"

Jade widened her eyes as if she knew what Serena planned to do. Serena wanted to say, "Everyone is a suspect until they aren't," but gave her daughter a radiant smile instead.

"Andre," Serena said, guiding him to the buffet. "Tell me about yourself. What got you interested in theater?"

"Oh." Andre chuckled. "It's just an elective. I chose it because I thought…"

"It would be easy." Serena finished his thought. "Got it. So, it's not your major. What is?"

"Marketing." Andre took a plate and piled five tiny sandwiches and four desserts onto it. "Sorry. I'm hungry." He held up the dish. "I'm starting my senior year in the fall, and hope an NFL team notices me. It's my dream to play in the big leagues."

"National football league." Serena smirked. *I was right!* "You play for the university. Are you good?"

"I think so." Andre popped a sandwich into his mouth.

"Just so you're aware, Jade is a freshman and has three more years ahead of her. I want her to finish college even though she'd love to…"

"Model." Andre pointed at her with a sandwich in his hand. "I agree with you one hundred percent, Ms. Tate. I promised my mom I'd get my degree no matter what happens."

Serena gazed at him for a moment, then said, "I have another question, Why join the gingerbread people? It wasn't a requirement of the class, was it?" *And you must be six-foot-three and stood out as the tallest gingerbread person I'd ever seen.*

"Not a requirement, but if I signed up, it would help my final grade. Meg, who is in charge, made a pitch during class, and the professor agreed to add points to our grade if we volunteered. I'd seen Jade and Jewel in the business department building and when they hung the flyer for the market, I was totally in." Andre smiled.

"You joined the gingerbreads to meet girls," Serena said.

"A girl," Andre corrected.

Serena was beginning to like Andre but pushed those feelings aside. "How well did you know Carmody? Did he have any enemies?"

"Carmody is…or should I say…was a gifted actor. He had unique ideas that set him apart from others. Some people don't like that."

"Were they jealous of him?"

"I don't know the theater majors as well as my teammates, but there's a hierarchy like in any group."

"Who is the leader? The mean girl?" Serena checked herself. *Am I asking these questions for the right reasons? Yes. Every bit of information helps.*

"Felix, the guy in the choir, is one of the leaders, and I'd choose Anna as a mean girl." Andre poured a glass of iced tea. "Would you like one?"

"Yes, thank you." Serena took the glass after he poured it and searched the area for Anna. "You've been quite helpful, Andre. Take a glass to Jade. I'm sure she'd appreciate it."

Weaving through the crowd, Serena finally chose a quiet corner table by the bathroom hallway. She retrieved her journal from her bag and scribbled down her insights. Yet the mystery remained elusive.

"Serena," Jack slid into a chair next to her. "Discover anything else?"

"Andre is off the list. He joined the gingerbreads so he could meet Jade. He's on the football team and has no interest in theater. Doesn't seem like the jealous type either." She swirled the ice in her glass. "On to our next suspect. Anna Wagner."

Chapter Sixteen

"I need to escape the madness, if only for a moment," Anna mumbled as she headed to the restroom.

Serena and Jack still sat at the table near the bathroom hallway. Serena glanced at Jack and widened her eyes. "She's upset," she whispered. "We'll wait for her to come out."

"Anna," Serena called to her as she came from the hallway. "Sit with us."

Anna wrinkled her brow as if deciding what to do. Finally, she took a seat across from Serena. "Is something wrong?" she asked.

"You appear stressed, and I thought some quiet time away from friends might help." Serena took a sip of tea. "Did you eat? The tearoom food is fabulous."

"I can't." Anna shook her head. "I'm overwhelmed and nervous. I don't like stressful situations."

"I'm sorry to hear that, but someone died," Serena said in a firm voice. "It's more than a stressful situation."

"I didn't word it correctly, but hope you understood what I meant." Anna eyed Serena's iced tea.

"Would you like one?" Jack asked. "I'll get a round for the table."

"Thanks, Jack." Serena loved how Jack recognized she needed alone time with Anna. She studied the girl, who was twirling a long blonde lock of hair around her finger. *Is she nervous because she killed Carmody or knows who did?*

"Now, Anna, besides Carmody's death, what else has you stressed out?" Serena used her most caring voice.

"Everyone." Anna huffed. "Felix, especially."

"Oh, guy trouble." Serena gave her a knowing look. "Are you a couple?" *So, it's Felix, not Carmody.*

Anna lifted her shoulder. "Sometimes."

"When it's convenient for him." Serena pursed her lips. "What about now?"

"Felix wanted to be included in Jade and Jewel's inner circle, so he pretended we were a couple again so we could hang out with them. Jade was in one of my classes, and we became friends."

"You believe Felix is using you," Serena said.

"Maybe?" Anna blinked back tears. "In a way, he is, but we dated on and off last year."

Typical drama. "Would you rather be with the group or alone with Felix?" Serena asked.

"It's okay either way. Felix likes the group atmosphere."

"What about Carmody? Did Felix get along with him?"

"I like Carm, but Felix doesn't. He and Carm avoided each other since the incident."

"Refresh my memory," Serena said.

"It was a stupid argument. Guys can be so dumb." Anna rolled her eyes.

Serena tried a different approach, hoping to get more information from Anna. "I'm going to visit Sunita at the hospital tonight." She watched for Anna's reaction. "If she is awake, I'd like to ask her some questions."

Anna appeared unfazed. "She's a good dancer and director. The troupe needs her back."

Jack returned with a tray of drinks and sandwiches. "Did you eat, Serena?" he asked.

Before Serena could answer, Anna took her tea and rose from her seat. "Thanks for tea, Mr. Ando," she said. "I'm going to find my sister."

"I hope I didn't scare her away," Jack said, returning to his seat. "Find out anything?"

"She likes Carmody. Felix is using her. They date on and off. Would she do his bidding or cover for him?" Serena struggled to recall a Felix and Carmody confrontation she was sure she'd witnessed, then remembered the incident from last week. In her mind, she pictured Felix pushing Carmody in the chest and telling him to back off. "Jack." She faced him. "In the security video, the masked elf pushed Carm in the chest. I need to watch it again."

"I have it right here," Jack said, wiggling his phone in the air. "Did you get an idea?"

"Yes, please play it." Serena watched the action until they got to the push. "Stop. This is the part I want to see."

After examining the footage, Serena said. "One more time, please."

"Obviously you saw someone push Carmody like this before." Jack pulled his brows together. "Who?"

"Felix. I need to find him." Serena sat straighter to get a better view of the room. "He has reddish-blonde hair and is about six feet tall. Not as slender as Carmody, but close enough to pass as the elf. Ooh, Jack, in my opinion, it's him. He killed Carmody."

"Not so fast, Serena. First, we need to discuss motive, means and opportunity. If Felix did this, I don't want you to approach him and tip him off."

"Okay, let's start with means." Serena opened her journal.

"Sissy, why are you hiding in this back corner?" Sasha approached the table and sat in Anna's chair. "Hey, Jack. Good to see you." She exhaled loudly. "I swear if I have to speak to one more police officer, I'll scream."

"The police are here?" Serena asked.

"After I spoke with you, I returned to the reception hall. They had set up a table and questioned people in groups of four. When the memorial ends, the kids are next."

"I wonder why they waited until almost four o'clock," Serena replied. "They should have started this morning."

"Lots going on," Sasha answered. "Especially since we heard the news about Sunita going to the hospital. The gossip went to another level in the reception hall." She locked eyes with Serena. "Do you remember our discussion about the nutcracker and the men's cologne?"

"How could I forget?"

"As I made my way over here, I passed by Felix."

"And?" Serena leaned forward.

"I swear he's wearing the same scent. He's your man."

"Or it's a coincidence." Serena didn't want Sasha revealing any information before she and Jack had a chance to investigate. Although she wouldn't tell her cousin, the news was huge. It confirmed what she had suspected. Felix might be the guilty party.

It appeared Sasha was done with their conversation. She had turned in her seat and appeared to be searching the area.

"Looking for someone?" Serena asked.

"Um…no."

"Justice." Serena leaned toward her cousin and stared at her, waiting for her to break.

"Okay," Sasha huffed. "He texted me. Asked me to save him from listening to gossip and stories about Carmody."

For once, Serena didn't mind if Sasha joined Justice. She and Jack had work to do. "It's fine. Go find him." She waited for Sasha to leave and turned to Jack. "What do you think? Is the men's cologne coincidence or a lead?"

"It helps the case but wouldn't hold up in court," Jack stated.

"A memory came to me when Sasha said gossip," Serena said. "I remembered what Jewel told me last week. Felix likes her and is jealous of Carmody."

"Motive." Jack tapped Serena's journal, signaling for her to start writing. "But kill him? If he is our suspect, I don't think he meant to harm him in that way."

"Maybe not, but don't forget Felix wanted to stop Carmody from reporting him." Serena wrote so fast she hoped she could read it later. "Contemplate this." She tapped her pen on the journal. "Felix decided to become the second elf when he noticed that Carm's behavior annoyed some people. He used the nutcrackers to get Carm in trouble, hoping Jewel would drop him."

"When Felix realized we accused Josef instead of Carmody, he knew he had to make Carm a suspect, too. So, he amplified the game," Jack explained. "When Carm swiped one of Maggie's pies, Felix made sure she got a nutcracker after she voiced a complaint."

"He must have seen Sunita's fight with Carm." Serena jotted down more information. "Felix has access to the storeroom and could easily steal a box of nutcrackers. That covers means."

"Opportunity is easy. He had full access to the market." Jack threw his hands in the air. "He dressed as Carmody when he delivered the nutcrackers. If someone saw him..."

"They'd blame Carmody." Serena high-fived Jack. "We did it."

"Wait a minute. It's all speculation. You're forgetting the most important part of solving the crime. Proof. We don't have fingerprints." Jack held up one finger. "Or a witness." He held up another finger.

"I'm positive we have a witness," Serena replied. "Why is Anna so nervous? The more I think about it, I believe she saw something. Who is the only person she'd protect?"

"Felix." Jack looked past Serena. "She's having a heated discussion with him now."

"I'm going to rescue her." Serena pushed back her chair.

"Be careful. Give nothing away," Jack said. "Tell her she left something at our table."

"Good one." Serena pointed at him, then wove through the crowd trying to look casual. "Oh, I'm sorry." She bumped into Felix. "I'm so busy looking for Anna, I wasn't watching where I was going." Serena gave Anna her best faux surprise expression. "There you are. Anna, you left something at the table."

Serena grabbed the girl by the arm before she could protest and steered her away from Felix. Anna struggled for a moment, then allowed Serena to lead her to the table.

"I couldn't have left anything," she protested.

Serena gestured to an empty chair. "Sit."

Anna slid into the seat. "I don't understand." She gestured to the tabletop. "See. Nothing here."

"Sorry, I had it wrong, Anna. You didn't *leave* something. You *saw* something," Serena corrected.

Anna squinted. "That makes no sense, Ms. Tate."

"Let me spell it out for you," Serena said. "Sunita reported someone had left a nutcracker for her before she arrived at the market. She brought you and Sophie to verify her story, which you did. But you, Anna, and perhaps your sister had seen the person responsible. You witnessed him fleeing the scene of the crime."

"The elf?" Anna wrinkled her nose. "I never saw him or anyone else."

"You're not a good liar, Anna. I should have realized you weren't telling the truth." Serena leaned against the back of her chair. "After you backed up Sunita's story, the elf left you a nutcracker as a warning. Instead of showing concern, you were ecstatic."

"I wouldn't say ecstatic. I liked it."

"Because you knew Felix had left it for you."

"What?" Anna blinked and widened her eyes.

"You thought he liked you again," Serena said in a sympathetic tone. "It was his way of showing you he still cared."

"Also, to make sure you didn't reveal what you had seen," Jack added. "You told Felix you saw him put the nutcracker where the dance troupe performed, didn't you?"

"How did you…?" A tear escaped from Anna's eye and rolled down her cheek.

"The hotel has security cameras in all its public places," Jack answered. "We have him on film."

Shocked that her upstanding boyfriend lied, Serena chimed in. "I saw the footage, Anna."

"He said he did it for fun." Anna hung her head. "I can't believe he killed Carmody."

"You keep saying he, Anna," Jack replied. "Who do you mean?"

Anna dropped her head and mumbled, "Felix."

"We've got our witness, Serena," Jack said and rose from his chair. "Anna, I must take you to the police station. You need to tell them what you told us."

Anna began to cry and covered her face with her hands.

"Jack," Serena whispered. "Remember what Sasha said? The police are here. It may be easier to take Anna to the reception hall."

"Hey, Serena," Mia said, as she and Lily approached the table. "We've been looking for you." She glanced at Anna. "Oh. Sorry. Are we interrupting?"

"Please, take our seats," Jack offered. "I'm taking Anna to the reception hall."

"Stay with her, Jack. She appears shaken," Serena said under her breath.

"Okay, but what about the hospital?" Jack asked. "You and I planned to go after the memorial."

"We'll go with her," Lily answered, gesturing to Mia as she chose her seat.

Serena loved her friends. Lily volunteered to take Jack's place without asking the reason. "I'll give them the details, Jack. We'll be fine," she said.

Mia leaned forward and whispered, "Anna looks terrified. Does she know who killed Carmody?"

"Felix," Serena answered. "Anna is our witness."

"No wonder she's scared. She's so young to be involved in a crime," Lily replied and held up her phone. "I messaged the valet service and requested a car to take us to the hospital."

"Do you want to visit Sunita?" Mia asked.

"If they will let us," Serena answered. "If not, there are ways around it."

"I'm good at distracting people," Lily said. She checked her phone. "Car's here. Let's go."

* * * *

"Wow, that was easy. They just gave us a room number and let us go," Serena said in the elevator. "It's a good sign. Sunita must be okay."

"This way." Lily motioned for Mia and Serena to follow her once they stepped from the elevator. "Room four-oh-four."

Further down the hall, Serena noticed a police officer standing outside a closed door. She nudged Mia. "I wonder what's going on there. Guarding a prisoner?"

"I have no clue." Mia took Serena's arm. "One mystery at a time, my dear friend."

Serena entered Sunita's hospital room, and to her surprise, found her sitting up in bed. "Sunita, it's good to see you are awake," she said.

"Serena and her friends. How nice of you to visit." Sunita struggled to sit straighter.

"Let me help." Serena adjusted the pillow behind Sunita's back. "You gave me quite the scare. What happened?"

"I overdosed on valium," Sunita replied with a shrug. "I don't have a prescription for it and never have taken it."

Serena glanced at Mia and Lily. "I saw Sasha earlier, and she had an iced tea with Sunita. Could someone have spiked Sunita's drink?"

"They could have," Sunita said. "I forgot the glasses on the table, and a person from the choir brought them to us."

"Male or female?" Lily asked.

"I don't remember." Sunita touched her forehead. "A few things are hazy, but I remember why I came to see you, Serena. I wanted to tell you who killed Carmody."

"Well?" Serena stared at her, waiting for the answer.

"Felix."

"I thought he did it, too." Serena pumped her fist. "You just confirmed it, Sunita. But we need more than your word."

"There is a witness," Sunita answered. "While I was getting drinks at the table, one of my dancers came to me in tears. She said she might have an idea of who killed Carmody and wanted my opinion. She had overheard the two sisters, Anna and Sophie, speaking about Felix. They saw him run from the scene of the crime."

"After he hit Carmody?" Lily asked.

"No." Sunita shook her head. "When he placed the nutcracker in the dance area."

Chapter Seventeen

Serena waited, hoping Sunita had more information. When she stayed silent, Serena replied. "Placing a nutcracker on the floor isn't illegal. That won't help us solve this crime."

"I believe it does," Sunita answered. "We needed the identity of this person, and now you have it. *Felix.* I'm not surprised one bit. He's complained about Carmody since the first day of the market, and he decided to get him in trouble."

You've complained about Carmody, too. "It's a start, Sunita." Serena sat on the edge of the bed and took Sunita's hand. "How are you feeling? I can pass along any message you'd like to send to your dancers."

"Tell them I will be fine," Sunita answered. "I'll get a good night's rest here at the hospital, and they'll release me tomorrow. Tell them I'll be back and ready to dance." She dropped her head and whispered, "If the market opens."

"We're not sure what will happen yet."

"I understand." Sunita nodded.

"I have a question," Serena said. "It's unrelated to Carmody or this case. Any idea why a guard is posted outside the room down the hall? Have you heard anything?"

Sasha's face brightened. "I heard the nurses talking. The doctor chose certain ones to attend to the person and swore them to secrecy. They bet it might be someone famous or a high-powered executive."

"Perhaps." Serena's curiosity grabbed hold of her and wouldn't let go. "Take care, Sunita. We'll see you tomorrow."

Exiting the room, Serena turned to Lily and Mia. "I want to see who's behind that door."

"Why?" Mia appeared surprised.

"I can't give you a reason, Mia. I'm going on pure instinct."

"I'm in," Lily said. "I'll distract the officer, and you go into the room."

"What about me?" Mia asked.

"Just look innocent." Lily told her. "Let's act like we're lost. We're three friends searching for your grandmother's room."

"Ooh, grandmother wouldn't like that," Mia teased.

"Then we won't tell her about our adventure," Lily said with a chuckle.

"She will find out," Serena replied. "Nina seems to know everything."

The women giggled as they continued down the hall.

"This way," Lily said in a loud voice, pointing to the left corridor.

"No, I swear Grandmother said to go right," Mia answered.

Lily approached the officer. "Sir? You probably know this hospital inside and out." She took his arm and turned him away from the door. "Which way to room four twenty-one?"

Serena turned the handle with great care and pushed open the door with her shoulder, until it allowed her to slip inside. What she discovered inside the room shocked her. A familiar young man lay in the bed. "Carmody?"

"Ms. Tate! Did you come to rescue me?" Carmody asked, although it sounded as if he was kidding.

"No." Serena blinked to make sure she wasn't imagining him. "I didn't know you were alive."

"People think I'm dead?" Carmody slapped the mattress. "Now it makes sense."

"Sense?"

"I was told I couldn't leave the hospital until the doctor gave his approval. All I have is a mild concussion and a few stitches in my head." Carmody pointed to the white gauze taped to the back of his head. "Although I heard there was a lot of blood. I woke up inside the ambulance and was immediately taken to this private room before I could speak with anyone."

"Detective Mitchell's orders?" Serena smirked.

"Yeah. He asked me a ton of questions. I couldn't help him. The elf dressed as me never spoke and wore a mask. I have no clue who it was." Carmody paused. "I told him the truth. I was looking for Jewel, saw your office door ajar and thought she might be in there. But I found an elf dressed like me instead. Imagine my shock. I told them

I would report my findings to you and that's when they gave chase."

"The detective hid you away and let us believe you were dead. He's determined to solve the case before I do," Serena replied with a shake of her head. "It's not a game. It's not a competition. He's pretending you're dead. To what means? What is wrong with that man?"

"Jewel thinks I'm dead?" Carmody widened his eyes.

"Everyone does. After they took you to the hospital, Jack contacted the station and learned you didn't survive."

"Can you get me out of here?" Carmody asked.

"I'll try."

The door burst open, and the officer entered. His angry expression said it all. "What are you doing?" he yelled. His neck turned red and the color flowed into his cheeks.

"I'm his mother," Serena said without hesitation.

"What?" The officer gazed at Serena, then he shifted to Carmody.

"I'm adopted," Carmody said. "Mom is here to take me home."

Serena bit her lip and willed every muscle not to shake with laughter. "Where is the doctor?" she asked. "I'd like to speak with him about my son."

"I'll be right back." The officer appeared confused and hurried out the door.

Serena turned to face Lily and Mia, who stood in the doorway. When they made eye contact, the three laughed until tears rolled down their cheeks.

"I wasn't aware you had a son, Serena," Lily teased.

"I do now," Serena answered. "And I have a plan. We need to discuss the details before we leave." She turned to Carmody. "You in?"

"To find my killer?" Carmody asked.

"Yes, and get them to confess."

* * * *

"There you are, Serena," Josef's booming voice made Serena jump as she walked into the hotel. "Just the person I wanted to see," he continued.

Josef took Serena by the arm and led her to his shop. "I heard you found Bernhard in your office."

"Who?" Serena wrinkled her brow.

"The clockmaker," Josef said. "Another one of my nutcrackers will safely come home after the police finish examining it." He lowered his voice. "Rumors suggest you know the bandit's identity. Is it possible for me to ask them a few questions? Alone in a locked room?" He pounded his fist into the palm of his other hand.

Serena widened her eyes and took a step back. "Um, no."

"Serena." Josef softened his voice. "I am only joking. Once we expose the scoundrel, they must reveal my box's location."

"I suppose he will."

"Oh." Josef arched a brow. "So, the killer is male."

"I didn't say that," Serena scolded herself for giving away a clue. "You must be patient, Josef. The police will reunite you with your stolen nutcrackers soon."

"I am confident with you on the case." Josef chuckled.

"Don't let Detective Mitchell hear you say that," Serena said.

"The man with the…" Josef made a rounded motion over his stomach.

"Yes, that's Bill Mitchell. Have you seen him?"

"He was in the reception hall until a few minutes ago. The detective rushed out of the hotel after receiving a call. We were told he had an emergency."

Good. The first part of the plan worked. Get Bill Mitchell out of the hotel. "Did it relate to the case?" Serena asked.

"You know the police. They'd never tell us. They only instructed us to stay in the hotel and do not leave," Josef answered.

"I won't keep you then. You should return to the reception hall," Serena suggested in a polite voice. *I don't want to hurt his feelings, but I must get going. I can't put the plan in place until I get to the tearoom.*

"One last thing before I go," Josef said. "Viktor would never murder someone."

"I don't know anyone named Viktor," Serena replied. "Are you trying to trick me into saying the actual name?"

"No." Josef shook his head. "I am speaking of my court jester."

"You named him Viktor? Not Chester Laughsalot or Chuckleberry or Whimsy Will?" *I should write those down.*

"What is wrong with his name?" Josef appeared offended. "It is a strong and valiant one. Jesters had to make kings laugh. Not an easy job."

"True. I'm sorry I questioned his name." Before she continued on her journey, Serena decided to confront Josef. "You didn't come here to sell nutcrackers, did you, Josef?"

"What?" Josef placed his hand on his heart.

"Germany is not exactly next door," Serena stated.

"I wanted to see the United States, and they offered free room and board. How could I refuse?" Josef answered. "San Francisco was on my bucket list, as they say."

"Since you learned Max lived here."

"No." Josef shook his head.

"Josef." Serena folded her arms over her chest.

"Alright. It was the reason I accepted the invitation. There. Are you happy now?" Josef raised his brows.

"Yes." Serena dropped her arms. "I like you, Josef. Thanks for coming and helping my girls, even though it wasn't the actual reason you came."

Josef grinned, reminding Serena of a cinnamon-colored teddy bear. "My pleasure."

"Now, if you'll excuse me?"

Of course." Josef dipped his head. "Thank you, Serena. You have helped me more than you know."

"Oh?"

"I let the past go. Max invited me to dinner last night and explained why he couldn't amend things. He is correct in his evaluation of our situation. We shall not be friends but not mortal enemies anymore. My life is good, Serena, and I intend to make the best of it." Josef put out his hand.

Serena shook Josef's hand, touched and impressed he had come to a formidable conclusion with Max. "It's wonderful to hear."

"I can tell you are eager to leave, Serena. I won't keep you, although I would love to treat you to dinner."

"So kind," Serena replied. "With all that's happening, I can't commit. I hope you understand."

"I will hold you to it." Josef chuckled, pointing a finger at her.

Serena took a different path, hoping Josef wouldn't follow. Making sure he left the area, she rounded back to his shop, stationed by the pond. Samurai emerged from the water and swam to the edge.

"Sam," Serena said. "Carmody is not dead. I'll tell you more later." The fish swam around the pond and leaped into the air. "That is how I feel. A happy holiday might be possible after all."

Serena had called Jack from the hospital to include him in their secret meeting. They'd assigned him the task of bringing the young adults back into the tearoom before Serena's arrival. Jack confirmed that the police had taken Anna's statement and promised to escort her to the restaurant.

Serena paused at the tearoom entrance, closing her eyes to savor the jasmine fragrance which greeted guests in the lobby. *Please let this work.* The sound of muffled voices drifted from the main room, assuring her that Jack had done his job. He was to inform the students that Serena had a major announcement, and they needed to gather in the tearoom. She opened her eyes, glanced upwards and murmured a brief prayer. "Here I go."

When Serena entered the restaurant, all eyes went to her. "Hello, everyone. Thank you for coming. I just returned from the hospital." She found the tables where most of the dance troupe sat and said, "Sunita is fine."

A loud cheer erupted, and Serena waited for them to settle. "It is good news, isn't it? Sunita sent you a message. She'll be here tomorrow and can't wait to see you."

"What happened to her?" One dancer asked.

"I will let her explain," Serena answered. "It's her story to tell." *If I mention valium, I might tip off the would-be killer.* "While I was there, I made a fascinating discovery. You won't believe this." She turned toward the entrance. "Mia? Lily?"

Mia and Lily walked into the restaurant with Carmody between them, holding his arms for extra support. The doctor had told Serena he would need someone with him for the next twenty-four hours in case he had a relapse.

Behind Serena, a piercing shriek sounded, followed by her daughter's touch on her back. "Is it him?" Jewel whispered.

"Yes, baby girl. It's Carmody." Jewel rushed past her and ran to Carmody. "Be careful," Serena called. "He just got out of the hospital."

"He's alive?" Felix screamed and covered his face. "I can't believe it." He dropped to his knees and looked up at the ceiling, putting his palms together. "Thank you."

"I didn't know you and Carmody were close," Serena said to the kneeling young man.

"We…aren't…I'm just happy he survived." Felix rose to his feet and approached Carmody, extending his hand. "Glad you're back."

"Are you?" Carmody snarled.

"What's wrong, man?"

"Great acting job, Felix," Carmody growled. "You try to kill me, then praise the heavens when I show up alive. Look at everyone else." He waved his hand across his body. "They are happy but don't appear relieved like you. Afraid you were going to prison?"

"What are you talking about?" Felix widened his eyes and shook his head.

"Let me," Serena said, slipping between Felix and Carmody. "Did you dress up like an elf, Felix?"

"Yes."

"Why? What was the reason?" Serena asked.

"I had two reasons. One. I thought it was fun. Two. I wanted to pin the pranks on Carmody."

"Why you…" Carmody took a step toward Felix.

"No, Carmody," Jewel shouted. "You're lying, Felix. I know the actual reason you wanted to make Carm look bad."

Carmody wrinkled his brow and cocked his head. "You do?"

"Yes." Jewel took Carmody's hand. "Felix asked me out before you did. I told him no, and I said yes to you."

"He was jealous," Serena said. "Jealousy can make you do drastic things." She eyed Felix. "Like hit someone over the head with a nutcracker and leave him for dead."

"I didn't!" Felix pounded on his chest. "Carm, I never would go that far…"

"So, you admit you stole the box of nutcrackers and gave them to people who perceived them as threats from Carmody?" Serena asked.

"Threats? No." Felix wrinkled his nose. "Pranks. I did it for fun."

"And to get Carm into trouble," Jewel said, placing a hand on her hip.

"I never thought of that until Maggie Potts complained to your mom, Jewel. I followed her to hear what she'd say," Felix said in a contrite voice. "I thought the apple pie routine was funny, but when I heard Maggie say he had no manners, it gave me the idea. I paid attention to who he interacted with throughout the day. Sunita was next. After I saw their altercation, I left her a nutcracker the next morning."

"Sunita brought Anna and Sophie as witnesses," Serena said. "You saw Sunita bring them in here, so they had to receive a nutcracker."

"Yeah, to keep it consistent and make people believe Carm was the prankster." Felix hung his head. "After our morning performance that day, Anna told me she saw me run from the gardens. I begged her not to tell and explained why I did it."

"Just for fun," Serena said in a deadpan voice.

"Exactly. It's the reason I bought the mask. I didn't want anyone else to identify me." Felix held up his pointer finger. "You forgot one prank. I left a nutcracker for Max, our musical director. He yelled at us and at Carmody, so he kind of deserved one."

The choir, who sat at different tables throughout the restaurant, chuckled in agreement.

"Did you forget one? I believe you left my office door ajar so you could leave a nutcracker in my office. Were you trying to scare me?" Serena asked.

"No. I never put one in your office. That was not me." Felix met Serena's eyes and held her gaze. "You've got to believe me."

Jack stepped forward, holding his cell phone. "This isn't you?"

Serena could see the security footage from where she stood. "Looks like you," she said. "Mask, gloves and same elf costume as Carmody. How did you find one that looks exactly like his? My friend, Mia, designed it."

"I can answer that," Mia said. "I had three sets made in case one got torn or needed washing."

"Anyone could have bought the same mask," Felix said. "I got it from a local store."

"The person I found in your office never spoke, Ms. Tate," Carmody said. "I can't say for sure it was Felix."

"Well. Well. Well. Look what we have here," Bill Mitchell's voice traveled through the tearoom. "You found my star witness, Ms. Tate. Bravo. Did he tell you he couldn't identify his attacker? Now you see why I had him under police protection until I discovered who tried to kill him. But don't worry about the boy, solving the crime is more important to you. I'll take it from here." He turned to the doorway and motioned for two officers to join him. "Arrest him," he said, pointing at Felix. "Read him his rights out in the gardens."

"No! Wait. I didn't do it." Felix struggled as the officers guided him toward the exit.

"As usual," Bill said to Serena and Jack. "Thanks for all your help." He paused and turned. "Take care of your *son*, Ms. Tate."

Chapter Eighteen

"You're letting him leave without a fight?" Jack whispered.

"Yes," Serena said, turning to him. "Bill Mitchell has the wrong person."

Jack widened his eyes at her statement. "Are you sure?"

"Yes, I'll tell you more, but first let's check on my daughter." Serena slipped her arm through Jack's and tilted her head toward Jewel and Carmody. "Isn't that cute? They're holding hands across the table."

"Mom!" Jewel rose from her seat to give Serena a hug when the couple arrived. "Carmody shared every detail from being knocked out until you rescued him from the hospital." Jewel giggled. "You said you were his mom?"

"Yes, and luckily, the officer didn't question me or ask for identification. It came as a shock to hear I was Carmody's mom. Besides, no one messes with someone's mother." Serena chuckled. "I recalled Carm being from out-of-state, so there was little chance of his actual parents arriving that quickly."

"Thanks, Ms. Tate," Carmody stretched out his arm to take her hand. "You saved me from Detective Mitchell."

"You're welcome." Serena slid her hand into his. "Jewel, Carmody will stay in my suite until tomorrow morning. The doctor said he needs constant supervision for the next twenty-four hours."

"I'll make sure he's okay," Jewel said.

"He's to rest on the sofa bed," Serena replied.

"Where will you sleep?"

Serena marched her daughter away from the table and said in a quiet voice, "In a chair next to him. You don't need to worry or keep watch. *I* promised to look after him."

"You are so sweet, Mom. I didn't know you cared that much about him." Jewel winked before heading back to her table.

"I'd help any human being in crisis, Ms. Jewel Tate," Serena called after her.

"We know." Jewel laughed and took Carmody's hand as she slid into her seat.

"He's growing on me," Serena said, pointing at Carmody. "As long as he behaves." She closed one eye and pursed her lips.

"I will." Carmody held up the scout's honor sign.

"Now that we've settled that…" Jack placed his hand on Serena's back. "Let's continue our discussion."

"Serena, my dear child," Nina said, as she suddenly appeared.

Serena never got used to Nina showing up unannounced. She'd look, and there she was. She swore the woman possessed magical powers, appearing and vanishing in a puff of smoke. "Nina, did Mia call you?"

"I came as soon as I could," Nina said, exhaling. "Thank goodness no one died." She glanced at the table where Carm sat with Jewel. "That boy, Felix, did not harm Carmody."

"How did you...?" Serena stared at Nina.

"I heard his confession."

"I should have guessed." Serena smiled at the woman. "When Felix locked eyes with me, I knew he didn't do it. He was truthful about all he had done and reminded me of the pranks I'd forgotten to mention."

"He left out the first one," Jack stated. "Sasha."

"True." Serena nodded. "But it doesn't matter because he didn't do it." She turned to Nina. "Have you made a decision about the market?" she asked.

Nina signaled for Jade to join her and said, "We will open the market tomorrow. The hotel has released a statement regarding Carmody's condition. We reassured people that the suspect who attacked him is in custody. We said it was a personal conflict between two market participants but will also increase security."

"Thank you, Mrs. Takeda," Jade said. "I prayed for a positive outcome for everyone. This is unbelievable." She glanced at her sister. "I'm so happy for Jewel, and that the police arrested the person who hurt Carmody."

Nina gave Serena a sideways glance. "Jade, sweetie," Serena said. "Could you get the group's attention? We'll let Nina tell them the good news."

"Sure." Jade went to Jewel's table and retrieved her sister. She urged her to stand next to her while she spoke.

"Everyone, listen up. Mrs. Takeda wants to make an announcement."

Nina gave detailed instructions to the performers in the room. "I have also given the same instructions to the vendors and entertainers in the reception hall. If you have questions, you can come to Ms. Tate. Whatever she says or decides is the final word. Understand?" She waited and only heard silence. "Good. Tomorrow is Saturday, so let's have a successful weekend." The room broke out into applause. "You are now dismissed." Nina bowed her head.

"She's clearing the room," Jack said to Serena.

"I'll make sure Lily and Mia stay," Serena replied and headed toward her friends.

"We're not going anywhere," Lily said when she saw Serena coming her way. "Mia ordered tea and food."

Serena wrinkled her nose. "There's no food left from Carmody's memorial?"

"The way those kids eat?" Lily shook her head. "Not much. Whatever was left, they took to the reception hall. I hope Jack likes quiche. I ordered two for the table."

"I got him eating cucumber sandwiches," Serena said. "He'll eat quiche."

The restaurant staff swarmed the dining room after it emptied. They cleared tables, wiped them down and realigned the lanterns to their centers. Jun escorted the group to their table in the far corner and said, "Tea is coming. Mr. Ando, I must say I am not aware of your preference."

"That's right, Jack, you've never joined us for a meal," Serena said, eager to hear his answer.

"Sencha, Jun, thanks," Jack answered.

"Very good, Jack," Nina said. "Sencha is a green tea, Serena. One of the most popular in Japan."

"It is the only one my mother makes," Jack replied. "I grew up drinking it." He paused. "With lots of milk."

The women laughed, and Serena loved that she'd learned something new about Jack. "Can I pour a small amount in my cup to taste it?" she asked.

"I will bring you another cup, Serena," Jun said. "And Jack, would you like some milk?"

Again, the table laughed, and Serena was grateful for the comedy relief, yet she couldn't stop thinking about the actual suspect. "I don't want to change the mood, but I must ask, who still thinks Felix is our person of interest? Anyone?"

No one raised their hand or spoke a word. "I hoped you shared the same outlook. Something told me Felix wasn't our guy, but he appeared guilty. Jack claims my only flaw as a detective is allowing emotions to interfere with the facts. I've been working on it."

"You have worked hard to not let your emotions take over, Serena." Jack agreed. "We all have learned from the behaviors of liars, cheaters and even killers. Let's give credit to ourselves. We can also recognize when someone tells the truth. At first, I thought Felix was guilty, then I changed my mind."

"I agree with you, Jack," Lily said. "Felix was so relieved to see Carmody, he appeared guilty. When he dropped to his knees, I thought we had our man."

"He must have known the police would eventually zero in on him," Mia said. "They could take the elf costumes and check them for DNA. Further proof against him."

"Oh, Mia, I love you," Serena exclaimed. "You gave me a great idea. That's how we get the person to confess. DNA. Now we need a plan."

"Before moving onto an actual plan, we must do means, motive and opportunity," Jack said. "We should start with motive. It will help us understand why she did it."

"She?" Nina arched a brow. "Why don't we call her by name? Anna Wagner."

"Alright." Jack faced Serena. "Is that who you suspect?"

"Yes." Serena looked at Lily and Mia who nodded in agreement. "We decided jealousy was the motive but forgot one person in the equation. Anna. A woman can sense a man's interest in someone else, even if she's dating him."

"Jewel said Felix asked her out," Mia said. "She must have told Anna."

"Jewel would only tell her if Felix and Anna weren't dating," Serena said. "I know my girl. She'd never hurt Anna's feelings."

"But then." Lily held up her pointer finger. "Felix showed interest in Anna again. She assumed he'd given up on Jewel when she started dating Carmody."

"Exactly," Serena replied. "Until Anna learned Felix used her to get into Jewel's orbit. Remember the security footage? Four couples entered my office. One was Anna and Felix." *Did they drink? Some can purchase alcohol due to their age. With all that's going on, I hadn't considered it.*

"Serena?" Jack touched her arm. "Are you okay?"

Serena shook her head to clear her mind. "I lost focus for a moment. I'm back." She let out a calming breath. "Anna is a smart girl. It didn't take her long to discover what Felix was doing. After speaking with her, I could tell she likes him. *Really* likes him. So, what's a girl to do?"

"Impress him," Lily said in an excited voice. "That's her motive. Jealousy took over, so she devised a plan. She would hide some nutcrackers, too, and show Felix she was just as capable. In her mind, they'd bond over their secret."

"Until Carmody caught her putting a nutcracker in your office, Serena," Mia said. "It scared her into doing something stupid."

"Like chase Carmody with the nutcracker she planned to give him as a prank?" Jack asked. "Instead, she planted it in the back of his head. Things got messy, and as I previously stated, the person panicked."

"I mentioned it could be a woman," Nina added. "Anna is tall and slender. She could easily wear something to disguise her bosom."

"Let's talk about the costume," Mia said. "I believe it falls under the category of means. Anna knew we kept the costumes in a storage room closet. She simply had to steal one when no one was looking. But what about the nutcrackers? How did she discover them?"

"Can I tell my theory?" Serena asked. "Once Anna learned Felix was the nutcracker bandit, she followed him to his hiding place. Simple as that. Anyone else?"

"She may have stumbled across them," Lily said. "But I doubt it. You're right, Serena, there's no other explanation."

"On to opportunity." Jack tapped the table. "Security footage shows four couples going to Serena's office after market hours. When the evening was over, Anna was the last to depart. She left the door ajar for easy access the following morning." He glanced around the table. "We don't need to call another market meeting. You three women should rehearse a casual conversation that Anna will overhear."

"About the costume and DNA?" Mia asked. "Sure."

"I'll have Jade and Jewel bring the sisters to my office where they can overhear us talking," Serena replied. "Anna might confess after hearing us discuss the DNA theory."

"No." Lily shook her head. "Anna must hear the news with all her peers in a public setting. It will make her feel guilty as heck, and she'll break down. Do it in the reception hall in front of everyone."

"Both are excellent ideas," Jack said. "What's your opinion, Serena?"

Serena took a moment to think. "We should go with Lily's plan. We'll have more witnesses, and Anna can't escape as easily." She paused. "Should we call Bill Mitchell and tell him to come?"

Jack nodded. "I'll speak with Sue Downing since she's the one who would check the DNA and have her pass along the information to Bill."

"Sue! We should invite her to speak to the group," Serena exclaimed. "This will give the meeting an official vibe."

"First, we need to video conference with Sue," Jack replied. "I'll call her."

"Serena?" Justice's voice came from the tearoom's entrance. "Can we talk?"

Serena placed a hand on Jack's arm. "Start without me. I'll speak with Justice and see what he wants." She joined him at the door and gestured to the empty gardens. "Let's go out there."

"Is it true what I heard? Carmody didn't die, and the police took Felix to the station for questioning?"

"Where have you been? Living in a cave? This is old news."

Justice hung his head. "In the bar. We had drinks to pass the time."

"We?"

"Sasha and I were bored."

"Oh, now it makes sense." Serena turned to go into the restaurant, and Justice grasped her arm. "Don't be jealous, baby. You had your chance."

"What did you say?" Serena struggled to get free of his grip and the smell of alcohol on his breath.

"I'm talking about you and me. You ruined everything," Justice said. "No one compares to you, Serena. Not even Sasha."

Serena closed one eye. "Did you tell Sasha that?"

Justice made a face. "No."

"How many women are you dating, Justice? Does this 'you're the woman for me' approach work on them? It's not for me."

"I'm not married, so I can date who I want, when I want."

"So, I'm right. You have multiple girlfriends. Just keep them away from your daughters," Serena huffed. "I need to get back inside."

"Okay, but one more thing," Justice said.

Justice tugged her closer, and Serena was an inch away from his mouth when she heard, "You heard the woman. Let her go."

Justice released his grip and smiled. "She's all yours, Security Guy."

Serena rushed into Jack's open arms. "How did you know to come?"

"The way he swaggered out of the restaurant. Was he drinking?"

"Yes…with Sasha." Serena leaned against Jack. "I'm okay. I can handle him."

"You can, but we're a team. I support you, and you do the same for me." Jack took Serena by the shoulders. "Let's talk about something else." He checked to see if Justice had left the gardens. "We haven't discussed Christmas."

"We're too busy solving mysteries," Serena said with a humorless laugh. "I figured you'd go to LA to see your parents."

"I will, but not before spending Christmas Eve with you." Jack kissed her. "That's when you plan to have your family party, right?"

"You have perfect recall," Serena said.

"I'll use the Takeda helicopter and fly into LA Christmas morning." Jack stared into her eyes. "I want to ask you something."

No! Too soon. Serena widened her eyes, hoping she was mistaken.

"My parents would love to meet you. The woman who stole their son's heart. Can you join us for dinner the day after Christmas? We'd come back to San Francisco together."

"Oh, Jack, that sounds lovely," Serena answered, relieved to hear the actual proposal. "Are you sure?"

"Never surer." Jack brought her close to him and whispered. "I love you, Serena."

"And I love you." Serena smiled and gave him a gentle kiss. Exhaling, she said, "I guess it's back to business for now. Right?"

"Right." Jack took her hand. "We contacted Sue, gave her the details, and she'll be here within the hour."

Chapter Nineteen

"May I have your attention?" Serena asked the people gathered in the reception hall. "Officer Downing wishes to speak to you regarding some important information." She moved away from the podium that the staff had hurriedly set up for the occasion. "You're on, Sue," she whispered as they passed each other.

"Hello, my name is Sue Downing, and I work for the San Francisco Police Department," Sue announced into the microphone. "We believe there are several masked elves and have taken the costumes to the station for further examination. I oversee the forensic team and will check each suit for DNA. We have Carmody's sample but need ones from market participants."

A protest went up in the crowd. "No!" someone shouted. "That's illegal," another said. "Why suspect all of us?" a man yelled.

"We can run your names through our database to see if you have anything on file and use those results," Sue continued. "If there's nothing on file, we'd prefer that you volunteer, but those who don't, we can get a warrant. You may hire a lawyer, but it might be time-consuming."

Josef raised his hand. "I volunteer. I have nothing to hide."

"Thank you, Mr....?"

"Bauer. Josef Bauer."

"My staff will set up an enclosed area to swab anyone's cheek who volunteers today," Sue said, giving a look of thanks to Josef.

"I will go second," Sasha said from her seat. She gazed around the room. "How long do you want to stay here? Once this is done, we can resume selling our goods at the market. Did you read the press release? We open tomorrow."

Murmurs of relief spread through the room. More people stood and agreed to the cheek swabbing. Max Gruber encouraged his choir to stand and volunteer as a group. A sad moan came from within the cluster of people as they rose from their seats.

"Max," Sophie yelled. "I believe my sister is sick. She's gone pale, and her lips are turning blue. She's having trouble breathing."

"I'm a registered nurse." Sue Downing called as she rushed to Anna's side. "Please, stand back. Give her some room." She took Anna by the wrist and felt her pulse. "Take a few deep breaths, Anna. Breath in through your nose and out through your mouth." She demonstrated the technique. "Water?" She checked over her shoulder, and someone handed her a bottle. "Drink this. All of it." She placed the open container in Anna's hand.

Serena approached the podium, urging everyone to be seated. "Let's give Anna a minute. I believe she has something to say."

Sue had taken Anna to the back of the hall, and Serena rushed down the aisle until she reached them. The color had returned to Anna's cheeks, and her breathing seemed normal.

"Panic attack," Sue whispered. "However, she still needs to see a doctor."

Serena sat next to Anna and took her hand. "Do you wish to speak, Anna?"

"Yes," she whispered. "You don't need to check the suits, Officer Downing. It was me." She gave Sue the saddest look Serena had ever seen. Her heart broke for the girl. "It all happened so fast. I didn't mean any harm." She looked up and said in a loud voice, "Did you hear me? I am the masked elf who hit Carmody. Not Felix."

Gasps of surprise went through the room. Serena heard a woman say, "I can't believe it." Another person said, "You think you know someone."

Anna searched the room until her eyes fell on Carmody. "I'm sorry, Carm. I was trying to impress Felix by pretending to be the elf. Instead, it turned into a prank that went very wrong. When you caught me in the office, you startled me. You said you were going to find Ms. Tate, and I had to stop you. Reason with you. But you ran so fast, I could barely keep up."

"But then Carmody stopped in the gardens," Serena said, recalling the video. "What did he say to you?"

"He threatened to have me kicked out of the market and whatever groups I belonged to at school," Anna cried. "I have a music scholarship and couldn't let that happen. I chased him further into the gardens, and he took a wrong turn. He had nowhere to go, so I caught up to him. I don't know what came over me, but I lifted the nutcracker and struck him with all my might."

"Did you think you killed him?" Serena asked.

"No, I hoped I had knocked him out, giving me time to invent a story." Anna dropped her head. "I planned to say he tricked me into meeting him there so we could be alone. I was so shocked when he kissed me, I grabbed the nutcracker he'd brought with him and used it to get away."

"The news of Carm's death took you by surprise. You couldn't use that story," Serena said.

"It's the reason I stayed quiet. No one could identify the masked elf."

"Until we focused on Felix."

"Yes," Anna whispered.

"You let the police arrest him," Serena said. "Did he deserve that?"

A tear rolled down Anna's cheek. "For a moment, I felt vindicated. He had used me, and I felt he deserved what he got. Over time guilt consumed me, but then I realized they would not convict him of murder. I thought hitting someone should fall into a misdemeanor category, so if they charged him, he'd get a fine or probation."

"Did you look that up?" Serena questioned.

Anna shook her head. "No," she said under her breath.

"What about Sunita?" Serena asked. "You've gotten this far. You may as well confess to drugging her. How did you do it? Where did you get the valium?"

"I also want to know," a man shouted.

Serena recognized the voice. Detective Bill Mitchell had arrived. She made eye contact and saw the fury on his face. *He doesn't like that I solved his case…again. If he did his job instead of trying to win.* Serena sighed.

Bill Mitchell pushed his way to the back row of seats where Sue had stationed Anna. He came to a stop, placed his hands on his hips and said, "Is this the young lady who committed the crimes?"

"Bill," Sue answered in a scolding tone. "This young *woman* shouldn't be bullied. She admitted to hitting Carmody and was just about to tell us about Sunita. Care to sit and listen?" Sue cocked her head toward an open seat.

"Fine," Bill grumbled and headed for the chair.

"Go ahead." Serena squeezed Anna's hand and held on for support.

"I…I overheard a dancer speaking with Sunita while I was working at the drink table. The dancer must have eavesdropped on a conversation I had with my sister and learned Felix was the masked elf. Sunita promised she would go to Ms. Tate's office after she finished her iced tea. The two had spoken for so long, Sunita forgot the drinks on the table."

"I've heard this part of the story from Sunita," Serena said. "Where did you get the valium?"

"My sister and I are having our wisdom teeth pulled during winter break. I picked up our prescriptions this morning. We are supposed to take the valium before our appointments."

"So instead." Bill rose from his seat, as if ready to give a lecture. "You dumped them into Ms. Patel's iced tea. Were you trying to kill the woman?" He stood in front of Anna with only a foot between them. "Did you research how many were needed to kill someone?" His voice grew louder. "Or did you simply mix all the pills in her glass and hope for the best?"

"I didn't have time to research," Anna sobbed. "I just wanted to stop her. Give me time to think."

"You are a dangerous girl," Bill said. "You committed a crime to cover up another."

"Excuse me." Carmody arrived, holding Jewel's hand. "I never identified my attacker, and I'm not sure it was Anna."

"Carmody." Serena met his eyes. "DNA will prove she is."

"Then I won't press charges. All I have is a few stitches and a bad headache," Carmody stated, touching the back of his head.

"You must press charges," Bill roared. "What's wrong with you?"

"Nothing, sir." Carmody glanced down at Jewel. "We thank Anna for confessing and understand why she did it. It's up to Sunita if she wishes to press charges. Go harass her, officer."

"It's detective and don't tell me what to do," Bill growled. He turned to Sue. "Time to go. Bring the girl with you."

"Bill." Sue took him by the arm. "Anna must go to the hospital first. I believe she had a panic attack but can't be sure."

"Fine." Bill threw his hand in the air. "Bring her straight to the station after you see a doctor." He wiggled a finger in Sue's face. "Stay with her the entire time. I don't want to take any chances of her getting away."

"What about the rest of us?" Sasha called from her seat.

"You're free to go." Bill waved his hand in the air as he headed for the exit.

* * * *

Throngs of people attended the market the next day. Serena wondered if they had come to gawk or inspect the scene of the crime. Despite her reservations, the atmosphere seemed festive with holiday tunes playing through the speakers placed throughout the gardens and the choir singing on the half hour. She signed more books than usual, wondering if customers thought they were more special since they bought them at the market.

"Don't forget to add the date," a woman requested. She turned to her husband and said under her breath, "This could be valuable."

Even though Serena heard the remark, she said nothing. Her holiday spirit had returned, and nothing could squash the feeling. Her aunt, uncle and Sasha would spend Christmas Eve at her house. They would be together as a family unit after many years apart. When the girls asked if Justice could attend, it didn't alter her sunny disposition. Serena agreed he could come. *I can't believe I said yes.*

Carmody decided to stay in California rather than fly home for the holidays, due to the cost. Jewel gave her mom a pleading look, and Serena couldn't resist. "The more the merrier," she had said, then suggested Jade invite Andre.

"We're going to have a houseful," Serena mumbled. "I haven't been home to help Mama decorate or bake."

"Did I hear my name?" Robin Baker stood in front of Serena.

"Mama! I'm sorry. I feel like I've neglected you." Serena hopped up and rounded the table to hug her mother.

"No need to worry. We've taken care of things. My brother and his lovely wife are staying at the house. They've helped me decorate and shop. Your Aunt Tina is thrilled to be celebrating with us. We baked up a storm." Robin took Serena's hands and said in a quiet voice, "I was over the moon to hear Carmody was alive, and The Pearl Hotel survived an event without a murder."

"Don't let Nina hear you say that." Serena checked the area. "She's around here somewhere."

"What's going to happen to that poor girl Anna?" Robin asked. "We do the dumbest things when we're young, don't we?"

"According to Jack, if Sunita presses charges, it could lead to felony charges and a prison sentence, with the possibility of her being convicted of attempted murder. That is the worst case scenario." Serena shuddered. "The girl was not thinking clearly." She looked past her mom. "Speaking of Sunita…"

"Serena." Sunita waved. "I'm back and good as new."

"I am glad to see you," Serena replied. "Have you met my mom?" She gestured to Robin. "Robin Baker meet Sunita Patel."

"I'm pleased to meet you," Robin said.

"Same." Sunita took Robin's outstretched hand.

"I heard someone drugged you, Sunita. Terrible thing." Robin shook her head.

"Have you heard the entire story?" Serena asked. "Felix pulled some pranks but wasn't the assailant who attacked Carmody and drugged you."

"Yes, the police told me," Sunita answered. "I went to see Anna at the precinct this morning, and it's the reason I'm late. I wanted to hear her side of the story and why she did it. Not just Detective Mitchell's."

"And?" Robin raised her brows and glanced at Serena.

"Anna wanted Felix's attention. If he took notice, they could join forces until the market ended. When Carmody caught her in the act, she panicked. But." Sunita held up her pointer finger. "It doesn't justify what she did. She intentionally hit him over the head." She let out a breath. "When she heard my conversation with one of my dancers, Anna said she panicked again. This was too much, and I couldn't give her a pass. I feel she needs to learn a lesson. It is necessary to impose some punishment."

Serena caught her breath before letting out a gasp. "I understand."

"A fine. Probation. Nothing major," Sunita continued. "I won't press charges until I've heard what's at stake."

"Anna will lose her scholarship, but I suppose she needs to learn a lesson," Serena said with mixed feelings.

"If you'll excuse me, I need to find my dance troupe," Sunita said. "But I came to thank you for helping me yesterday, Serena, and for your visit. It lifted my spirits."

"Lots of that going around," Serena replied. "Holiday spirit." She gazed at Sunita for a little longer than usual, hoping the words had sunk in.

After Sunita left the book-signing table, Robin nudged Serena. "You believe Anna shouldn't have to pay for what she did. Am I right?"

"What if it was Jewel or Jade, Mama? I wouldn't want their lives to be ruined."

"Remember, my dear girl, whatever happens to Anna is meant to be. I will pray she gets the lightest sentence and has learned her lesson."

"Do you think Sunita will press charges?" Serena asked.

"By the look on her face? Yes."

Chapter Twenty

"Mom! Grandma!" Jade skipped up to the table, giving them each a hug. "It's a wonderful day, isn't it?"

"We were just saying that, darling," Robin answered. "You have quite the turnout here. Your market is a success."

"I wholeheartedly agree," Jade said. "Guess what?"

Serena's stomach flipped. "Dare I ask?"

"Mom." Jade mimicked Serena, placing a hand on her hip to emphasize a point. "It's great news."

"Don't mind your mother, Jade," Robin said. "Tell us."

"Mrs. Takeda said if the week continues to go smoothly, we can do it again next year." The smile on Jade's face radiated with pride and joy.

"That's wonderful, Jade." Serena wrapped her arm around her daughter's shoulders. "For all you've done, you better get an 'A' in that marketing class."

The three women stared at each other for a moment, wearing huge grins. Then a sound Serena hadn't heard in days spilled into the room. Their simple laughter filled her heart with happiness, something she hadn't felt in a while. Jack joined the group, wrinkled his brow, then began laughing with them. Serena leaned her head on his shoulder, knowing he didn't have a clue what had set off the merriment and loved him for wanting to share their joy.

"Hey, don't leave me out," Jewel called from behind Serena and squeezed into the circle. "Guess what?"

"Oh, no! Not again," Robin declared, which made them laugh again.

Jewel gave them a puzzled look. "I just wanted to share the news. Jade and I received an 'A' in marketing."

"That came full circle," Serena said, wiping the happy tears from her eyes. "I am proud of you, girls. Well done." She broke from the group and tapped the table, which held her books, pens and giveaways of bookmarks and candy. "Time to close up shop and return to my duties as human resource manager."

"Let's hope you won't get any complaints today," Robin said with a chuckle. "The second week should be smooth sailing after the events of the previous one."

"Ooh, Mama, I like your confidence." Serena took Jack's hand. "Should we get back to work?"

"I'll see you Christmas Eve, Jack," Robin said. "I need to do some shopping now." She pointed at Serena. "Make sure he meets your aunt and uncle. They're around here somewhere."

Once inside the tearoom, Serena turned to Jack. "I'm scared."

"What? Don't tell me something happened."

"No, it's the opposite." Serena hung her head. "Everything is too normal," she whispered.

"Is that a bad thing?" Jack placed his hands on Serena's waist. "You believe, don't you?"

Serena wrinkled her nose. "In what? Karma? Fate?"

"Santa Claus."

"Yes, I do." Serena giggled.

"Then let him work his magic." Jack kissed her cheek.

"You convinced me," Serena said. "I'll only worry about my girls."

"Nope. Not even them." Jack shook his head. "They've become wonderful, mature women who handled this situation beautifully. Let them fly on their own, Serena."

"Fine." Serena folded her arms over her chest. "What about Sasha and Justice?"

"They're two grown adults who can do whatever they want. If you ask me, Sasha's a smart, worldly person. She can handle herself."

"Jack Ando, not fair. You're erasing all my worries," Serena exclaimed with a sigh.

"Merry Christmas, Serena," Jack said, pulling her to him. He was about to kiss her when he widened his eyes. "Oh, no."

"What?"

"Sunita is heading our way," Jack whispered.

Serena turned toward the woman, giving her best smile. "Sunita, what can I do for you?"

"Can we talk?" Sunita gestured to the human resource table.

"Sure. Step into my office." Serena hoped her joke would lighten the mood.

Once settled, Jack motioned for Eve to bring them tea. She had learned to read his signals, and Serena and Jack appreciated how much she helped them during the market. Besides the daily tip, they planned to give her a special gift—a plane ticket to anywhere she wished to go. After speaking with Eve about the upcoming holiday, Serena suspected she'd choose to fly home and surprise her family. *The best kind of gift.*

"I received a phone call from Detective Mitchell," Sunita said, nodding at Eve as she placed a cup of tea in front of her. "He wants to close the case before the holidays."

"Makes sense," Jack replied. "But he barely gave you time to think. Am I correct?"

"Yes, he said to take my time, and two hours, later he's badgering me."

"Sounds like Bill," Serena said under her breath.

"Did he tell you how he wants to proceed?" Jack asked.

Sunita let out a breath. "It appears he wants to throw the book at this young girl, and I want her to learn a lesson. It's her first offense, and she doesn't deserve the harshest sentence. This is the reason I wanted to talk to you. Is the detective more focused on his reputation than doing the right thing?"

"I can't speak for him, Sunita," Serena said. "Jack and I know he wants a promotion and solving a big case may help, but this one doesn't fall into that category." She looked at Jack. "He is always trying to impress Nina. For some reason, he believes she's best friends with the police commissioner and solving crimes at The Pearl would help his cause."

"True," Jack stated. "Even if Nina had the ability, she wouldn't tell the commissioner to promote Bill or anyone else. I don't know what is going on in Mitchell's head."

"Okay, I understand him a little better," Sunita said. "Now, I need your help with presenting my case to the detective. What words should I use? I've researched and discovered people can plead guilty to a lesser charge… but how?"

"I can write something down for you," Jack said. "Do you want Anna to serve time?"

"Not really. She's in the station's jail, so she's getting a taste of prison life," Sunita answered. "As I said before, I want a fine issued, probation and community service."

"We'll work something out," Jack said. "I'll speak with my connections at the station. Don't contact Bill until I get back to you."

"Thank you. I feel much better." Sunita finished her tea. "I'm ready to dance."

* * * *

The Merry and Bright Christmas Market wrapped up on the Saturday before Christmas Eve. After packing up their shops, participants declared the event a success. Despite the cleanup, the gardens still sparkled with holiday magic.

After the twins closed the storage room door for the last time, Nina surprised the market participants with a holiday party in the reception hall, complete with DJ.

The younger crowd danced into the morning hours, while Serena enjoyed sitting at a table with her cousin, Justice and Jack watching the fun. She didn't mind if Sasha wanted to date Justice, although she wondered how Sasha would arrange their dates since she lived in Paris. *Not my problem.* She took Jack's hand, remembering how he said Santa would work his magic.

Serena's mind drifted back to the final days of the market. She had made sure Carmody went for his follow-up appointment, where he received a clean bill of health. Her daughter had almost lost someone she cared about, and Serena's stomach tightened at the thought. Fifteen years after losing her dad, it still stung, and she didn't want Jewel to carry that awful feeling for the rest of her life.

Sunita had consulted a lawyer, and since this was Anna's first offense, the court had given her two weeks in jail with time served and six months' probation. She also had to complete one hundred and fifty hours of community service.

Since he had hurt no one or broken the law, the police did not charge Felix with any crimes. Serena hoped Anna would keep her distance from the young man and see this as a fresh start.

When Serena glanced back at the dance floor, she discovered Nina sitting in what she thought was an empty chair next to her. "Nina!"

"Hello, Serena. Are you enjoying the evening?"

"Very much. I can't thank you enough for all you've done. Especially this party."

"Nonsense. This is the fun part of life. The good stuff."

"Merry Christmas, Nina." Tears filled Serena's eyes. "What are your plans for the holidays?"

"Kal and I will spend time with the family on Christmas Eve. My brother's sons and their families live here and help run the hotel, so I don't need to go far." Nina chuckled. "We even live on the same floor. I believe Ken is having us for dinner. Or is it Koji? Ooh. I better check."

"Yes, you better." Serena giggled.

"My son Ben and his wife, who are Mia's parents, will attend, plus my daughter Hanna, her husband and daughter are also coming."

"Don't forget Mia and Kade," Serena added.

"Never." Nina smiled. "Then Kal and I will spend Christmas evening with six wonderful couples. Mia's friends."

"I've heard of the six notorious couples," Serena said. "Lily and Gabe are one of them."

"They are, and you have met Chase, if I recall," Nina said.

"The pilot."

"Yes, you will eventually meet them all." Nina winked. "Hopefully under better circumstances."

"The plane ride wasn't so bad." Serena pictured Chase in his captain's uniform, boarding the jet that took her and her kidnapper to South America. Throughout the ordeal,

Serena had felt safe, even with the person who had just killed a mobster's daughter.

Nina patted Serena's hand. "I stopped by to say happy holidays." She leaned across Serena. "You, too, Jack." She shook his hand. "Enjoy the rest of the night."

A slow song started, and Kal approached his wife, offering his hand. "May I have this dance?" He whisked her onto the dance floor, waltzing across the floor and out the door.

"That was magical and swoon-worthy," Serena said to Jack. She checked the room. "We need to say our goodbyes to Mia and Lily before they leave. We won't see them again before Christmas Eve." She spotted her friends at the bar. "Come on, Jack."

"Hey, you two," Lily said as Serena and Jack approached. "It's getting late, and Mia and I were saying we needed to find you."

"Here we are," Serena replied and threw her arms around Lily. "Have a good holiday, my friend. Are you going home to Colorado?"

"Gabe and I leave in the morning. We'll return late Christmas afternoon. Friends are flying into San Francisco and staying until New Year's."

"Sounds fun."

"It is," Mia said. "We want you and Jack to be part of it. Please keep New Year's Eve open. Come and meet our friends and welcome the new year with us."

"Jack?" Serena checked his reaction.

"I'm in."

Serena slumped her shoulders. "I forgot. You know them."

"Soon you will, too." Jack slipped his arm around her waist.

"We'll send you details," Mia said. "I love you guys." She spread out her arms. "Group hug?"

The women formed a tight circle, and Serena yelled, "Jack, get in here." She felt the warmth and love and stored the memory in a special place in her heart.

Chapter Twenty One

Serena had never seen her family room this full of people. Family, friends and strangers, who now had become friends, chatted and mingled with each other. Her tree overflowed with presents, and she wondered how long it would take to open the gifts. Despite her willingness to party until the wee hours of the morning, she understood others had prior commitments.

"I want to give my gifts first," Robin announced. "Jack and Serena, will you please come forward?"

"So formal, Mama," Serena teased.

Robin pointed to the floor, and the couple sat as Robin placed the boxes in their laps. "Open together."

Serena glanced at Jack. "Okay. One. Two. Three. Go." She peered inside the box and burst into laughter. "Oh, Mama. I love it. It's quite appropriate as well." She pulled a woman nutcracker from the box. It held a book in one hand and a pencil in the other.

"She's an author," Robin said. "Not a teacher. Josef did the best he could to note the difference."

Serena examined the book. "Oh!" It bore the title of her first book, *Marry Me Never*, on it. "I love it."

Jack removed a Japanese samurai nutcracker from his box. "Wow! This is outstanding."

"Josef does excellent work," Robin said. "He followed my precise instructions. Check the back of his coat, Jack."

Jack flipped the nutcracker over and caught his breath. "My dragon tattoo. How did you…?"

"I have my ways." Robin chuckled.

"These are wonderful gifts, Mama," Serena said. "Also great keepsakes from the market."

"Stay where you are, Mom and Jack," Jade said. "Jewel and I want to give our gifts."

After Jade handed her a package, Serena wrinkled her nose as she gazed inside the large gift bag. "I have a feeling there's a theme tonight," she said, pulling tissue off the clockmaker nutcracker.

"How could you *not* have *thee* Clockmaker?" Jade cried. "After you solved the mystery and murder attempt, you needed to have him."

"We can laugh about it now," Serena said, pointing to the nutcrackers. "They serve as a lasting reminder of what might have been." Serena nudged Jack. "Your turn. I can't wait to see what you got."

Jack unwrapped an Asian Santa Claus nutcracker and nodded with approval. "I like him. Thank you, girls."

"You're our…" Jade stopped mid-sentence.

Serena realized whatever Jade was about to say would hurt Justice's feelings. *Time to save the day.* "Mom's lover!"

she shouted, causing the room to go silent. *Nope. Not what I planned to say.* "Whoops." She gazed up at Jade. "Would you mind giving Grandma my gift? It's right there." Serena pointed.

After opening another nutcracker, the festive mood returned. Who would get the next one became the running joke of the evening. Carmody gifted Serena with a new court jester since the original remained as evidence at the police station. Justice and Sasha even exchanged nutcrackers.

"That really cracks me up," Serena said, after they opened their presents. "Get it? Cracks? Nutcrackers?"

"Mom." Jewel rolled her eyes, and everyone laughed.

As the evening ended, Serena didn't want to say goodbye. She knew her family had Christmas morning ahead of them with her aunt, uncle and cousin, yet the night held a magical vibe. Just like Jack promised.

Serena walked Jack to the door. "You're going straight to The Pearl?"

"Yeah, I texted the pilot, and we'll takeoff in an hour. Merry Christmas, Serena." Jack's lips curved into the best smile. "I love you." He kissed her, then slid along her cheek, planting more as he went. When he reached her ear, he whispered, "I'll miss you."

"I'll see you in two days," Serena said.

"Two long days," Jack replied.

"Jack, I want to tell you something before you leave."

"Ooh, this sounds serious."

"It is. I found Jade alone in the kitchen and asked what she was going to say before I interrupted. I hope you know why I did it."

"You were thinking of Justice," Jack said.

Serena closed her eyes and gradually opened them. "Jade was about to say you are our hero. Our protector. You keep us safe from harm. You've restored her belief that someone other than her mom will do that. She thanked me for stopping her because she realized it's a father's job to protect, and she would have hurt Justice's feelings." She paused. "Jade said she almost forgot he was there. She sees you as a second dad."

Jack's cheeks turned rosy, and his eyes brimmed with tears. "I'd do anything for you and your family. I love those girls like they're my own."

"Aww, you're blushing." Serena touched his cheek. "I feel the same, Jack. You said to believe in Santa and the magic of Christmas. You are the best gift he could have stuffed down the chimney, Jack Ando. I love you."

Her other hand went to his opposite cheek, and she stroked them with her thumbs. "A lot has happened this year. Through the good and bad, you've been there for me."

Jack's lips captured hers, and Serena returned his kiss with equal passion. She didn't want him to leave yet knew she must let him go. Her heart was full of love and the holiday spirit, and she didn't want to lose it. "Don't leave. Not just yet. If you do…?"

Jack placed a finger on her lips. "Don't say it. Keep the magic in here." He pointed to her heart. "We'll talk tomorrow?"

"Let's Facetime while we open presents with the family." Serena knew she asked too much. "No, be with your parents and brother's family. Forget I said that."

"We'll work something out," Jack said. "Besides, I don't know how much sleep I'll get. My brother and his wife have a new baby."

"What? Why didn't you tell me?"

"We were kind of busy," Jack replied. "I also missed the birth announcement text, so I feel bad. He's a month old already."

Serena closed one eye. "When did you finally read the text?"

"Two weeks ago?" Jack grimaced.

"Looks like I've got some shopping to do before I arrive," Serena said.

"I see the excitement in your eyes," Jack replied.

"New babies do that to me." Serena poked him. "You said a boy, right?"

"Yes, a boy." Jack embraced her. "Now I'm really going."

"Take care, Santa," Serena said, giving him a lingering kiss. "See you in two days."

* * * *

The day after Christmas, Sasha rushed to get ready for an early flight to Paris. Serena accompanied her to the front door and said, "We've spent little time together, Sissy."

"Next year," Sasha answered.

Serena raised her brows. "You're coming for Christmas?"

"Yes, thanks to you. You made me see what I've been missing. Family and sharing the holiday with others. Besides, I signed up to take part in the next Christmas market."

"What?"

"Yep. I heard it's going to happen. See what you started?"

"I didn't. My girls are responsible for its creation."

"But you helped them. You got me here, right?"

"I'm beginning to think it was a mistake," Serena teased. "You fought off men the entire time you were here. The family barely saw you."

Sasha stuck out her lower lip. "I can't help that men fall in love with me wherever I go. First, it was Josef. Then…"

Serena held up her hand. "Don't say it. Did Justice say he loved you?"

"Yes."

Serena fought back the urge to tell her about his many secret girlfriends. "Do you plan to invite him to Paris?"

"Justice would love that," Sasha exclaimed. "But no. I don't have enough bedrooms for his other girlfriends."

"You know?"

"I wasn't born yesterday, Sissy. When Justice said he loved me, I got him to confess that he has other women in his life."

"When he proposed, I did the same thing." Serena high-fived her cousin.

"He's lost, Serena. I feel sorry for him," Sasha said.

"Sorry enough to let him come to Paris?"

"Ooh, my car is here." Sasha embraced Serena and whispered. "Justice is a player. I showed him the door and closed it with a bang. Happy New Year."

* * * *

"We finally get our last present, Jewel," Jade said, following Serena and Jewel into The Pearl's gardens. "Did you hide it somewhere in here?" she asked.

"It's not hide and seek," Serena answered. "No more questions, Jade. You've been nonstop since we got in the limo."

December twenty-sixth had finally arrived, and Serena's excitement continued to grow for two reasons. The girls' surprise, and she'd leave for LA in a few hours. She and the girls had shopped most of the morning, buying holiday bargains for baby Kody. She had at least learned his name and weight. "He's a butterball," Jack had said.

Not knowing much about Jack's parents, she had chosen a soft seafoam green throw for his mom and slippers for his dad after texting Jack for his size. She'd found a cute Christmas tote for Jack's brother and sister-in-law and filled it with baby clothes and toys. Satisfied, she'd ushered the girls to the waiting limo and headed to the hotel.

Serena admired the ruby and diamond tennis bracelet that sparkled on her wrist. Jack had given it to her Christmas Eve after everyone had left. Realizing ruby was her birthstone, he made sure to include them. She ran her fingers over the bracelet, feeling a connection to him.

"Mom," Jewel pointed at the pond. "Why are we stopping here?"

"This, my dear, sweet daughters, is your gift." Serena watched as the girls wrinkled their noses. "Stop." She waved a finger in front of their faces. "You have no idea what it is yet. Please step up to the railing."

"Samurai?" Serena said a little prayer, reminding herself it was just a fish. *But he promised!*

The women stood in silence and stared into the water. The sound of the fountain seemed louder than usual, as if laughing at Serena. A kaleidoscope of colored fish swam past them underwater—orange and white, gold with black speckles, white ones with black spots and some solid colors, but not a red and white one.

"How long do we have to wait for your imaginary fish to arrive?" Jade said in an exasperated tone. "I have plans."

Jewel leaned against the railing, checking her phone.

"Girls!" Serena blinked back tears. "Sam must sense you don't believe. He can see you're preoccupied with other things."

"Aww, Mom, don't get upset." Jewel slipped her phone into her purse. "I'll try harder."

"So will I." Jade rested her elbows on the railing. "Hello down there. Samurai?"

A red-headed koi poked his head out of the water.

"Sam!" Serena exclaimed. "It's him, girls."

"He's beautiful, Mom," Jewel said. "Can I see your tail, Sam?"

Sam swam in a circle and flipped his white-tipped tail in the air.

"That was a coincidence, right?" Jade pointed to the water.

"No. Ask him anything, Jade. Remember, heads means yes, and tails means no."

"Do you know my mom?" Jade asked. Samurai dove underwater and popped up his head. "Too easy." She laughed. "Here's a harder one. Am I Jewel?"

Samurai's head went into the water, and his tail shot high into the air. The girls continued to ask questions, getting the correct answer every time.

"Mom, this is so unbelievable. He really does exist," Jewel said. "Thanks for sharing Samurai with us. It was a wonderful present." She hugged Serena. "You made this an unforgettable Christmas."

"Yes," Jade said, joining the embrace. She leaned back and gazed at her sister and mom. "What do you think the new year will bring?"

Serena broke into a huge grin. "New beginnings?"

"Yes, let's agree to that," Jade said.

Serena led her daughters to the bench, put an arm around each of them and exclaimed, "I'm so lucky to have you."

Samurai sprung from the water, seeming to agree.

As they watched Samurai perform, the girls snuggled against Serena like when they were little. She hugged them tighter.

"Because of you, my precious ones, we had the best holiday. Your crazy idea of a Christmas market brought the family back together again."

"Crazy?" Jade looked up at Serena with one eye closed.

"Okay, not so crazy." Serena chuckled.

Serena kissed Jade's forehead and did the same to Jewel. "Merry Christmas, my sweet girls, Merry Christmas."

The End

Before You Go

Join Nancy's Mailing List and never miss a release!
Nancypennick.com

THANK YOU FOR READING

Did you enjoy this book?
I invite you to leave a review at your favorite book site,
such as
Goodreads, BookBub and Amazon.

DID YOU KNOW THAT LEAVING A REVIEW…

Helps other readers find books they may enjoy.
Gives you a chance to let your voice be heard.
Gives authors recognition for their hard work.
Doesn't have to be long. A sentence or two about why
you liked the book will do.

Continue Reading –

**The Pearl Hotel Cozy Mystery Series
(Cozy Mysteries are stand-alone reads)**

The Model's Last Pose (Book 1)
Gone with the Pearls (Book 2)
The Notorious Nutcracker Case (Book 3)
The Fatal Bouquet (Book 4)

Other Books by Nancy Pennick

The $ecret Billionaire $ociety
(Contemporary Romantic Suspense)

Chase (Book 1)
Nash (Book 2)
Finn (Book 3)
Beau (Book 4)
Gabe (Book 5)
Kade (Book 6)
The Elusive Mr. Smith (Book 7)
Smith's Revenge (Book 8)

The Billionaire's Bride
(Contemporary Romantic Suspense Series)

Vanessa (Book 1)
Grace (Book 2)
Charlotte (Book 3)
Tess (Book 4)
Lily (Book 5)
Mia (Book 6)

The Clan MacLaren Series
(Historical Romance)

My Highlander Husband (Book 1)
Donnach's Daughter (Book 2)
The Heart of the Emerald (Book 3)
Now and Forever (Book 4)
MacLaren Strong (Book 5)
Homecoming (Book 6)

ABOUT THE AUTHOR

For three decades, Nancy taught elementary school. She'd written short stories as a child, kept a diary and loved the writing process. After retiring, she hadn't set out to become an author, but when inspiration struck, she couldn't resist putting pen to paper. She now had time to follow her dream. Today her writing spans various genres, including young adult, historical romance, romantic suspense and cozy mysteries.

Nancy lives with her husband, Ron, and has a married son, who helps her with tech more than he likes! Plus, add in a wonderful daughter-in-law and grandson which makes her life complete.